The Ascendants

By Christian Green

January 2016

Published by

Legacy Press
Aurora, Illinois

ISBN: 978-0692618684

Acknowledgements

Special thanks to: Mya, Mizenburg, Wil, Donovan, Marc, Jenni, Kara, the Wolfpack crew, Richland second grade, the students of Ms. Kuhn's class and Rhonda for their excellent assistance and feedback; mom and dad, and of course every single one of you out there that has shown support for me during this incredible journey!

Chapter 1

One of Many

Cooper Barrett walked down the middle of the street without a care in the world. Onlookers stared in disbelief as the building behind them blazed from the fire he caused.

As Cooper walked passed the neighbors, he could feel their stares and hear their whispers. The attention he received did nothing but boost his ego. "Get out of the street!" a driver shouted out of his window. He honked the horn three times, but his aggressive demeanor didn't bother Cooper in the slightest.

The driver revved on the gas in an attempted warning, but still, Cooper paid him no mind. Out of frustration, the driver shook his head, pressed his foot on the gas and gunned it forward. He headed straight for Cooper, who had his back turned on the driver. When the car got within range, Cooper sidestepped to his right and evaded a collision. He pressed his hand on the hood of the car and almost instantaneously, the hood disintegrated.

"What the?" the driver shouted. The driver slammed on the brakes as hard as he could. He stepped out of the car and made his way towards Cooper.

"Problem?" Cooper asked with a slick smile. "Yeah, I got a problem, you just did something to my car!"

Cooper looked passed the driver and over towards the car. He found the damage he caused the car to be amusing.

"I would say I'm sorry, but I'm really not." The driver glared at Cooper and said something foul just before he took a hard swing at him.

"Well, that wasn't very nice," Cooper said as he evaded the driver's attempted attack.
The driver cursed again and positioned himself for another attempt.

"Oh please, don't even bother, there's nothing you can do to stop me."

Cooper's own words brought forth an epiphany, and he turned to face the growing crowd of bystanders. "There's nothing any of you can do to stop me!"

The crowd looked at one another with confused expressions.

"What's going on out here?" someone unaware of what just occurred asked.

A middle age man pointed right at Cooper. "That freak just melted half that car with his own hand. He's one of those freaks, one of those Post Humans!"

Cooper looked in the man's direction and grinned. "What you have just witnessed is nothing more than a small example of what I can do. I am here today to show you, to show all of you, that the world is changing. No longer will people like me hide in the shadows."

"I'm just trying to get to work. I could care less about any revolution or whatever nonsense you're talking about!" the driver of the disintegrated vehicle said.

Cooper chuckled. "Do you think your job is important? What I can do is important, what I am is important, what I represent is important!"

"And what exactly do you represent?" an authoritative voice asked.

Cooper looked around in an attempt to locate the source of the voice. A tall, slender, dark-skinned man dressed in all black and carrying heavy artillery stepped forward. Within seconds, three unmarked SUVS joined the scene, and multiple men dressed in the same all black attire stepped out of the vehicles and aimed their weapons at Cooper.

For a split second, Cooper's relaxed demeanor changed ever so slightly. "Your response time was unusually quick, and I don't recall ever encountering a team dressed like yours. Who are you?"

"Who I am isn't important, what is important is that you follow my instructions implicitly," the dark-skinned man said.

Cooper looked around and saw he was surrounded. "I don't take orders, not from the likes of you."

The dark-skinned man had a mixed reaction. He took the comment personal knowing the response was loaded.

Cooper smiled mischievously, "I'm sorry, did I offend you? This is quite the situation we have here. It seems that you are in quite the pickle."

The men surrounding Cooper all laughed together.

"We've got you surrounded. You're the one that's in quite the pickle," the lead agent said. Cooper grabbed the driver and placed his right arm across the man's throat and his left arm clutched the driver's right arm. "You might want to rethink your position."

"Let him go."

"I don't think so. You aren't in any position to give out demands."

The dark-skinned man looked towards the rest of his men and nodded. They responded to his head gesture by inching their way forward and moving in closer towards Cooper.

"Stop moving!" Cooper shouted. "Do you see

that car? Take another step forward and you'll suffer the same fate."

The dark-skinned man held up his left hand and balled it into a fist, a gesture that caused the other armed men to stop in their tracks and wait for instructions.

"You need to let this man go immediately." Cooper looked around the street and smiled. All eyes were on him and he loved it. "Soon the world will know. Let today serve as a warning. Let today serve as an awakening. We are the Chosen and our time is now!"

Cooper took his right hand off the driver and placed it on the driver's chest. Within seconds a large hole became visible in the middle of the driver's chest and he collapsed to the ground dying instantly.

The crowd screamed out in absolute shock at the site.

"Civilian is down, I repeat, civilian is down," the dark-skinned man said. "That's it boys, take him out!"

Cooper raised both his hands over his head and slammed them back down to the ground. The impact of the Cooper's attack caused the ground to shake and the weapons to fall out of the men's hands.

"Get him!"

Cooper used the distraction to aid him in his

escape attempt. He ran through the crowd and pushed through anyone that got in his way. As he neared, several of the civilians parted like the red sea. No one wanted to be anywhere near him.

"Move, move!" one of the armed men shouted to the crowd as he and the rest of his team moved after Cooper.

#mindblown! One onlooker posted on her MyFace page. Within minutes of the altercation, hundreds of videos, each with millions of views surfaced on the internet.

Cooper ran as fast he could from the armed men. The neighborhood was unfamiliar to him and as he tried to cut through one alley, he realized he had walked into a dead end.

"Freeze, don't move another inch!" one of the armed men shouted. The rest of the group closed in on Cooper. He had nowhere else to run.

"Do you have him?" the dark-skinned man asked over the radio dispatch to the rest of his men.

"Yes sir, Agent Hardine, we've got him trapped."

"Good, I'm on my way."
Agent Hardine got inside one of the SUVs and the driver took off down the street.

"Not so chosen now after all are you?" one agent asked.

Cooper stayed cool and smiled. "My capture is irrelevant. I am just one of many, the revolution cannot be contained, and even worse for you, it cannot be stopped. Surrender now and I'll make sure you are spared."

"Is this guy for real? What a joke!" one of the agents said.

"He's on something," another replied.

Seconds later Agent Hardine's SUV pulled up. "Cuff him."

The agent he spoke to looked at him hesitantly. Agent Hardine gave the man the hardest of looks. "Never mind, I'll do it myself!" He reached to his backside and pulled out a pair of handcuffs.

"Handcuffs? The situation is so much worse for you if you truly believe handcuffs is the answer," Cooper said. He laughed as Agent Hardine approached.

Agent Hardine wasn't too confident that the handcuffs would be enough to contain Cooper, but he saw no other options. "Don't move!"

"Standing still sir," Cooper mocked.

"Slowly put your hands behind your back."

Cooper moved slower than necessary for no reason other than to annoy the agent.

Just as Agent Hardine was about to apply the cuffs on Cooper, he found himself lifted off the ground by an invisible force and hurled into two of his fellow agents.

"Sir are you okay?" one agent asked.

"I'm fine, what the heck happened?"

The agent looked towards her right and pointed at three individuals. "Sir, I believe they happened."

Agent Hardine got to his feet and stared at the two individuals that approached his position. "Who are they supposed to be?"

"No idea sir."

The three individuals wore matching dark blue leather uniforms. Each individual had a holster for their weapon by their waist and another holster by their leg.

"Are these guys with us?" one agent asked as he noticed the similarities between their uniforms and that of the unknown individuals.

"Mission details didn't mention anything about another task force assisting," Agent Hardine said. Agent Hardine stepped forward and pointed his weapon at the trio. "That's far enough, identify yourself."

A small petite woman, with short stylish black hair to her shoulders stepped forward. "My name is-"

"Mia, they don't need to know your name," James, a man with biceps almost as large as Mia said.

"James, these guys will never trust us if we keep secrets from them," Mia said.

"Hate to state the obvious, but everything about us is a secret," said Cayde Brady, the third member of the trio.

Agent Hardine took another few steps forward. The rest of the agents followed suit. "I said state your name."

"Well, you said identify yourself, the second time you said state your name," Cayde said to be humorous. His sarcastic nature might've been tolerated by his peers, but Agent Hardine was less than amused.

Mia Rivera stepped forward. The attractive young woman had an innocent look about her which she often used to ease the tension between others. "We are the Ascendants."

Agent Hardine gave the group a hard look.

"You know, when you say the name out loud, it does sound somewhat intimidating," Cayde whispered to Mia.

Mia rolled her eyes. "Shut up Cayde." She turned her attention back to Agent Hardine. "We are here for that man."

"Well, what a coincidence, we're here for him too. As a matter of fact, we're here for people just like you."

James Payton reached to his side and pulled out a custom handgun. He shifted his weight and aimed the weapon at the agents.

"James!" Mia shouted. She kept her eyes locked on Agent Hardine, but stepped in front of James to prevent him from firing on the agents. "This is not the way to make friends!"

"News flash sweetheart, I don't think he's trying to," Cayde said.

Mia rolled her eyes. She looked around the area and noticed all the worried faces. She knew their terrified stares were directed at her and the rest of her team. All she ever wanted was to be normal, but she was far from it, and there was nothing she could do about it. "We don't mean to cause any trouble, but it's our responsibility to stop people that use their abilities to harm others."

"Is that right? It's your responsibility? On who's authority?" Agent Hardine asked.

Mia tried to think of a smart answer to reply with, but she knew nothing she said would matter to the agent.

"As I thought, enough of this. Drop your weapons or we will drop you."

Mia sighed. She had hoped that her team would've arrived on the scene earlier so they could've avoided the confrontation they faced.

"Can you please hurry up and get this over? My patience is running thin," James said through gritted teeth.

Mia shook her head and made a frustrated sound. "Fine, but you realize all of this could've been avoided if we would've left when I suggested, right?"

"Really? You want to have this conversation

right now?"

"I'm just saying." Mia flicked her hands forward and with a strong invisible force, knocked the weapons out of the agents' hands.

"We got a Post Human with telekinesis!" Agent Hardine said over the radio dispatch.

The agents attempted to grab their guns, but Mia used her telekinesis to control the weapons. She guided the weapons upwards and out of their reach.

Cayde watched in awe as Mia defied logic. Without ever touching the guns, she manipulated her hands in such a way she controlled all the agent's weapons. She turned the floating objects on the agents and held them hostage.

"I never get tired of seeing that!" Cayde said to James.

James smirked. "It is impressive; I'll give her that much."

Mia looked back towards James and Cayde. "Umm guys, yeah, I'm not going to be able to hold these weapons in place forever. Would you be a doll and grabbed the criminal?"

James nodded and moved forward in Cooper's direction. The agents sized him up and contemplated making a move.

"Are we really going to let this guy just take him?" one agent mumbled to Agent Hardine.

"Don't see too many other options here Agent,

how about you?"

The agent declined to reply as he knew Agent Hardine's question was rhetorical.

Cooper watched as James approached him. "I have to say, out of all the things I saw happening today, running into you guys wasn't one of them."

James grabbed Cooper and jerked him forward. "Yeah, well I wouldn't get too comfortable if I was you. You might find where you're headed to be less accommodating than anything they had in mind for you."

Cooper did not give James the satisfaction of a reply. He looked around at everyone and smirked.

"Don't even bother trying to disintegrate my arm or anything, the suit will absorb it," James said with a grin that matched Cooper's smirks.

Before Cooper could reply, James nailed him with a right hook that rendered him unconscious. Agent Hardine stood still, startled, and confused by James' actions.

Cayde held out his right arm and pressed a button in the center of a small band attached to his wrist. "We've got him."

"Copy that," a voice from the device replied. James lifted the unconscious man over his shoulder and worked his way away from the agents and back over to Mia.

Sweat trickled down from Mia's face and James knew she would not be able to hold the weapons in place for much longer.

"Well ladies and gentlemen, it's been a real pleasure, but it's well passed time for us to take our leave," Cayde said.

The churning sounds of a large ship caught the agent's attention. They all looked towards the sky as a massive vessel made its way towards them.

"They have a ship?" an agent said.

"It would appear so," Agent Hardine replied. He shook his head and cursed as frustration and disbelief overtook him. He had no choice but to watch the three individuals leave with his prisoner.

"I'm glad no one had to shoot each other today, oh and remember, we aren't the bad guys!" Cayde said.

Once everyone was on the ship, Mia released her hold on the weapons and they fell to the ground simultaneously.

"Fire on that ship, bring it down!" Agent Hardine ordered once his men regained their weapons.

The agents retrieved their weapons and fired, but the vessel was too far away to do any damage.

"What in the world just happened?" one agent asked.

"We got outmaneuvered," Agent Hardine said. He stood still and stared at the ship until it was out of sight.

"Sir, what do we do now?"

Agent Hardine did not respond.

"Sir?"

"We find out everything we can on these Ascendants. I want to know who they are, what they can do, and most importantly, where they are!"

The agent nodded in understanding.

"Do it now!" Agent Hardine said. His dark-skinned face turned a couple shades red.

"Right away sir."

The cell phone in Agent Hardine's pocket rang. He reached inside, took it out, and sighed when he saw the name on the other end. Agent Hardine swallowed spit and reluctantly answered the phone.

"Sir?"

"You've got some explaining to do. Meet me at headquarters immediately."

Agent Hardine could not get out another word before his superior ended the call. Agent Hardine placed his phone back into his pocket. He walked back to his SUV and waited for his driver to open the door. Agent Hardine got inside and sat in the passenger's seat. He cursed loudly as he prepared himself for what he knew to be a most unpleasant conversation.

Chapter 2

Remnants of the Past

"How's our guest?" Dr. Connors, leader of the Ascendants asked. He watched Cooper via a camera feed that linked to several big screens in the control center of the ship.

"Agitated," Christine Mercer replied.

"Well, I think I'd be pretty agitated too if James knocked me out," Cayde said.

Christine and Dr. Connors turned around to face Mia, James and Cayde. Christine did her best to hide her emotions, but she was quite pleased to see that the team returned safely. "You guys were reckless, that could've gone much smoother."

Cayde held his hands up in a defensive manner and pretended to be offended. "Well excuse me, I'm sorry we can't all be as efficient in the field as you are. Anytime you want to stop playing pilot and take to the ground, I'd be happy to trade places with you."

Christine laughed. "As if anyone would ever let you fly."

"Hey, I've logged in my hours, I know how to fly this baby."

Christine's eyebrow raised slightly. "Never said you didn't know how to fly, I said that no one in their right mind is going to let you fly it."

Cayde gave Christine an annoyed look. He turned towards Dr. Connors to see if there was any truth to Christine's statement.

"So, anyway, tell me about our guest," Dr. Connors said in a not-so-subtle attempt to change the topic.

"Cooper Barrett, age twenty-eight from Upstate New York. Cooper can disintegrate anything he touches. He uses his abilities in a destructive and deadly way," Christine said.

"He also mentioned something about the Chosen. Not sure if that's some sort of group or just his delusional thoughts of being special," James said.

Tommy Boyd, the team's resident computer genius and weapons expert rolled his chair over to his laptop and crunched away on the keyboard. "The Chosen, there's been a lot of chatter from a website called *WeAretheChosen.com.*"

Tommy grabbed a small rectangular remote next to his desk and projected the website on his laptop to the big screen.

Dr. Connors studied the images. There had to have been thousands of articles all of which contained news regarding Post Human activity.

"Tommy, what am I looking at exactly?"

"Umm, well if I had to guess, I'd say you're looking at Hitler reincarnated," Cayde said.

Dr. Connors rolled his eyes and ignored Cayde's remark. He kept his attention locked on Tommy and waited for a reply.

"Yeah, what Cayde said is pretty accurate," Tommy said.

"Thank you Tommy. Finally, there's someone willingly to acknowledge my brilliance!" Tommy crunched away at the keyboard and opened a back door into the website's hidden files.

Dr. Connors huffed.

"Basically, WeAretheChosen is a website designed to recruit Post Humans to their cause. The owner of this site believes Post Humans are the rightful inheritors of Earth. He or she is determined to prepare as many Post Humans as possible," Tommy said.

"Prepare them for what?" Christine asked.

"War," James replied.

Tommy shook his head in agreement. "This website has gotten millions of views and over twenty thousand registered members. This group could be a real problem."

Dr. Connors stared at the screen. He had heard rumblings of such an organization, but never did he imagine the reach the organization had. Dr.

Connors placed his left hand over his face and rubbed it. He sighed as he contemplated how to proceed with the findings.

"How do you want to handle this?" James asked.

Dr. Connors did not respond immediately. He needed to be sure his next course of action was the right one. "What about our new friends within the government, what do we know about them?"

Dr. Connors looked at Christine for an answer. The tall blonde Amazonian built woman had plenty of experience with analysis and profiling. She worked with the CIA for seven years, but went underground after someone she trusted dearly, betrayed her trust. She was supposed to have been brought in for "questioning," but Dr. Connors and James arrived just in time to rescue her.

"Not much at all sir. The guy in charge is named Kevin Hardine or Agent Hardine. He did two tours in Iraq before returning home to work for the FBI for five years. He's dedicated, highly trained, and a natural born leader. I think it's safe to say these guys are some sort of special opts unit."

Dr. Connors soaked in Christine's words. "Makes sense. We figured it was only a matter of time before the government created some sort of agency to combat these threats. What we need to determine now is if this agency is here to lock up all Post Humans or only those that abuse their abilities."

"You're thinking Holocaust right?" Cayde asked.

Dr. Connors and everyone else turned to face Cayde. Dr. Connors had an unsure look upon his face. "What?"

"Have you all been paying attention? There's real fear out there. People don't trust us. People don't like us. You know it's just a matter of time before some administration gives the order to round us all up. It may not be this administration, but it's coming."

There was silence in the room. Cayde's words struck a chord with the group.

"You sound like the sort of idiots spreading their fear through this website," Tommy said.

"Tommy's right. People like this Cooper Barrett and members of his organization pounce on fear. They take a person's apprehensiveness, their lack of understanding and they press on it. They use a person's fear to spread their agenda, to spread their hate. You can't think like that Cayde; you have to rise above it."

Cayde stared at the website. He walked over to the screen and pointed at one of the videos. "Take a look at this. Where was this video shot?

Somewhere off the coast of Costa Rica, right? There's a man that brought down a mountain just by slamming his hands together. Or how about this one, I see a man that just lifted a truck and threw it into a building? This is all real, and incredibly dangerous. I'm not saying I believe in what The Chosen are preaching, but I am saying there's many that will. We have to get on top of this situation before the entire world is against us."

There was another long silence in the room.

"You're right," Dr. Connors said.

"Now that's something you don't hear too often!" Christine said. She looked over to Cayde and stuck her tongue out at him.

"You can stick your tongue out at me any time you want love," Cayde said. Cayde pressed his lips together and blew Christine a kiss.

Christine rolled her eyes and contorted her face. Although she never wanted any harm to come to him, there were times that she just wanted to sock him in the face.

"All right, we've got two missions to handle. First thing we need to do is interrogate our new guest."

Dr. Connors looked around the room. "Speaking of interrogating, what's the status on Susan?"

Tori Hathaway closed her eyes and

concentrated. While she possessed no offensive abilities, her presence on the team was extremely valuable. She was perhaps the most valuable member of the team. One of her primary abilities, and the one the team used the most was her ability to track down any Post Human just by thinking of them. "She's in China sir."

"China?" Dr. Connors echoed.

"Should've known she'd take this assignment as an excuse to visit her family," Cayde teased.

"Do you want me to bring her in?" Tori asked.

"No, no need. If she's in China, I'm sure she's got a good reason, but that means you're going to have to do the interrogating."

Tori had an unsure look on her face. Being able to locate dangerous Post Humans was one thing, but Tori didn't like to be in the field. She didn't like to be anywhere near the dangerous ones.

Dr. Connors looked over towards James. "You'll go with her. I want you two to find out any and everything you can on this Chosen organization."

"Understood." James looked in Tori's direction and smiled. He walked over to her and placed his arm around her shoulder. "Come on kid, we've got this."

Tori rolled her eyes. "I'm seventeen James, I'm not a kid!"

"Yeah, yeah, just keep moving!"

Dr. Connors watched Tori and James walk out

of the control room, and then he turned his attention back on the rest of the group.

"As for the second mission. We need to find this agency and make it clear that we aren't a threat to them or national security."

"Well that sounds like fun, how do you suppose we accomplish that?" Cayde asked.

Dr. Connors looked over towards Christine.

"What? Why are you looking at me?" she asked.

Dr. Connors smiled. "Because this is your area, analysis and profiling are some of your strongest attributes. I'm confident you'll figure something out."

Christine sighed. "I'll see what I can do."

Dr. Connors nodded his approval. "Excellent, let's get to work."

Chapter 3

Two Missions One Goal

"So how do you want to play this?" Tori asked. Unlike Susan, Tori wasn't familiar with leading interrogations. In fact, just about everything she was involved in was new to her. Just a year ago, she was living at home with her parents, going to school, dating boys, and attending cheerleading practice. Never did she imagine that she would interrogate some of the world's biggest criminals just one year later.

"There really isn't a play so to speak. Just go in there and find out as much about this guy as you can," James said.

Tori sighed. "It's not that easy you know."

"What isn't?"

Tori stopped walking. "Using my abilities. There's nothing easy about it. Every time I activate it, my head gets dizzy."

"Yeah, I know the feeling. It wasn't easy for me either when I first started using mine."

"Did it hurt?"

"Not at first because of the adrenaline, but after time sets in, my bones felt like they had been run over by a truck."

Tori always enjoyed talking to James. Even though he was a hothead at times, he was still the easiest in the group to talk to. James never judged any of them and he always found a way to relate.

"What if this was the plan?"

James raised his eyebrow. "What do you mean?"

"I'm saying, what if we were meant to have these abilities? That it wasn't random. What if these abilities were given specifically to us?"

James pondered Tori's question. He had thought of it before, but never really took time to consider the answer. "If we were meant to have these abilities, why then are there so many that abuse them?"

Tori chortled slightly. "That's easy silly. Balance and free will. I think that every Post Human has their ability for a specific reason. I wish I understood it better."

"Yeah, well, let's just hope that whatever that specific reason was has nothing to do with the complete annihilation of Earth."

Tori looked at James with an uneasy expression.

"Yeah, I hope so too."

James walked passed Tori and blocked her entrance into the containment room. "You ready for this? I can take the lead if you're uncomfortable."

Tori took a deep breath. "No, I've got it, I have

to make a contribution to this team somehow."

James was surprised by Tori's self-doubt of her worth to the group. "You're kidding right? All of us are here because of you. If it wasn't for you Christine would've been locked up in some facility. If it wasn't for you, Cayde would've been in the morgue."

Tori looked around uncomfortably. When it came to being credited for her efforts, she had a hard time accepting the praise.

"If it wasn't- your gift is the reason we're all here and every Post Human we saved is because you led us to them." James paused and took the former cheerleader by the hand. "Hey, kid, don't ever think for one second that you aren't important."

Tori blushed. "Thanks James. And James-"

"Yeah?"

"Stop calling me kid!"

James laughed. He nodded and agreed not to call her that again. He swiped his hand over a motion sensor panel configured only to activate on an Ascendant's swipe. The door opened slowly and the two Ascendants walked in.

Cooper stared at the two individuals and a slick smile formed in the crease of his lips.

"Hello Cooper my name is Tori."

James' face revealed nothing, but he wasn't pleased with the fact that Tori had given her name. That made for the second time that day a member of his team had given their name away. He made a mental note to discuss his displeasure on the topic at a later time.

Cooper stared at Tori. Even though she was only seventeen, he couldn't help but noticed her attractiveness. Five feet, four inches, long blonde hair, slender frame, that was outlined by fine curves and a face that met the typical standards for what was attractive in the world.

"I'm a member of the Ascendants and I'm here to ask you a few questions."

Cooper laughed and looked towards James. "You can't be serious. Don't tell me she's your group's interrogator!"

James kept his massive arms folded across his chest but said nothing in reply to the man.

"I certainly hope she's not, because if she is, your group is way out of your league when dealing with me."

Tori looked towards James. Part of her agreed with Cooper's remarks.

"Get on with it," James said while he kept his stone cold face locked on Cooper.

"You two would be better off switching roles. You know, let the big guy play the bad cop and the little girl play the hot cop."

Tori gritted her teeth. "Let's get started!"

Cooper kept his eyes on Tori and smiled. He loved to get under people's skin, especially those he could control and manipulate with ease. "Okay, what do you want to know?"

Tori looked towards James who nodded back to her. "Okay, who are the Chosen?"

Cooper yawned. He walked back over to the bed and laid in it. "I'm sure by now you already know. I'm thinking now you've had enough time to Google the phrase on the internet. Did you like what you saw?"

"I'll be asking the questions here." In the corner of Tori's eye she could see James give a slight nod, a subtle admittance of his approval.

"Okay little lady, if that makes you feel important, by all means, ask away."

"How many members are in your organization?"

Cooper shrugged his shoulders. "Too many to count. All you need to know is that we are everywhere. You cannot fathom the extent of our reach."

"What's your goal?"

"To make this world a better place."

Tori seemed surprised by Cooper's answer, but she realized their versions of a better place was vastly different.

"Did I surprise you? We both want the same thing. To live in a world where we aren't feared. To live in a world where we don't have to be afraid of our gifts."

"How do you plan to make this world a better place?" Tori asked.

Cooper smiled with approval. "Now that's a better question. It's simple, the human race will have to get on board. Either they submit to our command or we will make them submit."

"How will you make them submit?"

"I'm sure you can use your imagination to figure that one out."

"How?" Tori repeated with a raised voice. Cooper ignored Tori and looked at James. Cooper had a wide grin on his face, one that was too wide to be sincere. "Do you see what I mean? Little girls are too emotional; they aren't cut out for this kind of work."

"Careful, she's just getting warmed up." James remained stoic in form.

"Tell me what I want to know or I will make you tell me!"

Unable to hide his amusement, Cooper laughed hysterically. There was nothing about Tori that intimidated him. To Cooper, Tori was nothing more than a teenage girl trying to act like a grownup.

"Don't say I didn't warn you."

"Oh so you're tough huh? Well I'll tell you what, open this containment field you got me locked in and let's go a few rounds. I mean I don't really like to hit women, but if you're so tough, let's see what you got."

Tori smiled and shook her head. "Okay, you really want to see what I got?"

Cooper nodded. Tori looked over to James who also nodded.

"Very well."

Tori closed her eyes and concentrated. Suddenly, Cooper screamed out in excruciating pain. He dropped to the ground and grabbed his head.

"What are you doing to me woman?"

"Oh, so now I'm a woman huh? Not such a little girl anymore am I?"

A smile sneaked passed James and showed on his face. He took great pleasure in Cooper's discomfort.

"My head, it feels like it's going to explode!" Cooper shouted.

"Just relax, it'll be over soon," James said.

For over three minutes Cooper felt the most agonizing pain he ever experienced. He wasn't the only one to wither in pain. Tori too experienced a similar level of discomfort as she read Cooper's mind. James moved over and placed himself behind Tori. He grabbed her shoulders and held her in place.

Finally, Tori's eyes opened, and she released her mental hold over Cooper. She fell backwards and landed safely into James' arms.

"Telepath," Cooper said once the interrogation was over. He squinted his eyes and slowly made his way to the bed.

"You guys are monsters!" Tori said. James gently released her and she stood upright on her own.

"I got all that I could from him. He's nothing more than a foot soldier," Tori said.

Tori didn't say another word to Cooper. She walked right out of the room and leaned up against the nearest wall.

"Not so little after all," James said to Cooper. He didn't bother to wait for a reply. He followed Tori out of the room and allowed her to lean on him until she could regain her composure.

"It's worse than any of us thought."

James sighed. "Let's head back to the control room. You can fill us all in at once."

James and Tori made their way back towards the rest of the group. Dr. Connors watched the entire altercation through one of the camera feeds and had already recalled the rest of the group to join him.

Tori and James entered the room, and Tori immediately took a seat. "I need a minute."

"How is she?" Dr. Connors asked.

"Shaken up, but she'll be okay. Locating Cooper and reading his mind certainly took a toll on her, but she's tough. She'll be just fine."

Mia walked over and handed Tori a bottle of water while Tommy took up a seat next to her.

"Are you okay?" Tommy asked.

"Yeah, I'm fine," Tori said.

She waited for Christine and Cayde to stop arguing over whatever pointless subject they were disputing. It must've been the millionth argument between the two.

"The Chosen is a group of Post Humans employed by a much larger entity," Tori said. Dr. Connors looked around at James and Christine. With Susan being off on assignment, those were the individuals he confided in the most. "What sort of entity?"

"The kind that can destroy entire countries using technology, cybering, economics, and Post Humans," Tori replied.

Dr. Connors looked worried.

"Okay, why don't you start from the beginning," James said.

Tori nodded. "The Chosen is an off shot of a much larger organization called the Syndicate. The Syndicate has thousands of people in their employment. They have departments in pretty much every area needed to run a special opts organization. Think CIA, FBI, CTU, all of them rolled into one."

There was complete silence in the room.

"The Syndicate is determined to take over the

world. They represent no one country and they have eyes and ears everywhere. The presence of Post Humans has done nothing but strengthen their position. The Chosen locate Post Humans and either bring them into their organization or kill them."

"How do they decide who lives and dies?" Christine asked.

"Anyone that offers any resistance and whose value isn't extremely high is killed immediately. They have Post Humans broken into three categories. Alpha Level, Beta Level and Low Level. All low level Post Humans they capture are killed, the rest are given a chance to prove their worth and their fate is determined by their evaluation."

"Who runs this organization?" Dr. Connors asked.

Tori had no decisive answer for Dr. Connors.

"Oh he knows, he just isn't telling you," Cayde said.

Again Tori shook her head left and right. "He didn't tell me anything, because he doesn't know. Trust me, I read his mind, there was no name."

Christine moved forward towards the computer monitor and press away at the keyboard. "Compartmentalization."

"Compart a mental what? That was quite a mouthful!" Cayde said.

Christine rolled her eyes at Cayde.

"Compartmentalization, it's a strategy big companies use. Especially the military and shadow groups. No one person sees the entire picture that way no one person can give everything away."

"No one person but the leader of this organization. We need to find out more about this group. Tori, is there anything else you can tell us?"

Tori searched her thoughts. She wished she could've provided more, but she had extracted all the information she was going to get from Cooper. "No sir, I don't have any other answers at this time."

"You don't, but perhaps I do!" Christine said. She pressed the remote near her monitor and pulled up her screen on the control room's big screen.

"What is it?" James asked.

"Using Tommy's tracking program I did a scan for any captured images of Cooper. The program captured his image thirty-two times within the last month on camera, of those thirty-two times, seven were with this man."

Christine pointed to the image of a lean, but well defined image of a man on the screen.

"Who is he?" Dr. Connors asked.

"No clue, but-" Christine walked back over to her computer and searched her desktop. She located the icon she was looking for and clicked on it. "Running facial recognition now. With any luck, we should have a hit soon."

Dr. Connors was pleased to hear that. "Tommy, take over for Christine, and tell me as soon as you find something."

"Roger that sir."

"Roger that? Tommy, this isn't the military!"

"Yeah I know, but I've always wanted to say that!"

The group shared a laugh. Dr. Connors looked towards Christine and gestured for her to follow him. She looked back at the monitor, double checking to make sure the program ran properly. Satisfied, she left her station and followed Dr. Connors through the hall.

"I saw the look on your face when Tori mentioned the Syndicate. Anything you want to share?"

Christine hesitated. "Nothing concrete, but I've heard mentions of the organization in passing."
"Really, how come you've never mentioned it to any of us?"

"Because it was nothing more than office talk."

Dr. Connors raised an eyebrow. "Office talk, you mean you heard of this organization back in your days with the CIA?"

"Yes. Like I said it was mostly just office talk. Anytime there was something that couldn't be explained or something horrible happened that no organization took credit for, people would say it was the Syndicate."

Dr. Connors sighed. "Well, it's safe to say there's some truth to that office talk, and if it's anything close to what Tori described, we could all be in serious trouble."

"Agreed, let's see what the program turns up and we'll go from there."

"What about the other mission? Did you turn up anything on this government agency that's been tracking down Post Humans?"

Christine pressed the power button at the top right corner of her tablet. She swiped left to disable the lock and pulled up a file.

"Right after James, Mia and Cayde left the scene, Agent Hardine dialed a number. I had Tommy run a trace on the number and we got a hit. The man Agent Hardine contacted is Commander James Sullivan. He served in Vietnam and did a tour in Iraq and Afghanistan. I never served under him but I have met him on several occasions. He's a company guy. Falls into command without ever wavering and hardly ever questioning his superiors. He's superb at what he does and his trust is very limited. Approaching him won't be easy."

Dr. Connors hung his head. "This day seems to be getting more frustrating by the minute."

Christine smiled. "I said it wouldn't be easy, not impossible."

"What do you have in mind?" Dr. Connors

asked.

Christine swiped through a couple pages on her tablet and pulled up another file. "I had Tommy hack Commander Sullivan's cell phone and activate the phone's GPS. As long as that GPS is on, we can track Commander Sullivan wherever he goes."

Dr. Connors was impressed. "I knew Tommy was good with electronics and engineering, but I had no idea he could hack into phones like that."

"He's a genius sir. Tommy can pretty much hack into anything. I'm sure he could hack into the pentagon and the white house too if he wanted."

Dr. Connors raised his hands. "Let's not get too far ahead of ourselves. Hacking into a government agent's property is bad enough."

Christine smiled. "Just saying."

Seconds later James popped his head into the hallway where Dr. Connors and Christine conversed. "We got something."
Dr. Connors and Christine looked at each other and then followed James back to the control center.

"We got a hit?" Dr. Connors asked.

"Yep, don't know how much it'll help, but I've definitely got something."

Dr. Connors stared at an image displayed on the screen.

"His name is Dorian Granier sir. Not much on file about him. He's thirty-five years old and from Boston, Massachusetts. There hasn't been a job listed for him in the past five years' sir."

"Any family?"

Tommy flipped to the next page. "No sir, no family."

"At least, no family listed," Christine said. The group turned to face her. "If he's connected to the Syndicate like we suspect, there's a strong chance that aspects of his life would be unknown."

"Especially if he's high up the chain," James added.

Cayde had a perplexed expression upon his face. "How could information like that not be available?"

"It's actually relatively easy to conceal information if you know about the finer workings of coding. Take us for example. If anyone pulled up a basic report on any of us, our files would look similar."

"Really?"

"Yep, one of the first things I do whenever we find someone that needs protection is delete the majority of their files."

Cayde found himself impressed and bothered at the same time. Even though he was only in his late twenties, he wasn't as knowledgeable with the internet as one would expect.

"All right you two, let's stay on task. So this Dorian Granier, hardly anything on him besides the very basics. Tommy, can you hack into his phone and get a track on his location?" Dr. Connors asked.

Immediately, Tommy shook his head. "I've already tried. There's no number for him listed. Unlike Commander Sullivan, this guy doesn't seem to be in possession of a cell phone."

Cayde raised his hand. "And what all do we know about this Commander Sullivan fella?"

"He's the leader of the agency you ran into earlier today," Tommy said.

Cayde rubbed his head and pretended to have a headache. "Too many names and organization being thrown at once. This is quite confusing!"

Christine rolled her eyes. Over the past year she had developed quite the love/hate relationship towards Cayde. James often teased her about her feelings, much to her chagrin. "It's really quite simple. We're dealing with two completely separate organizations with two different agendas. The first organization we ran into is led by a man named Commander Sullivan, who I believe works for the government."

Tommy paused to let the group process the information. "The second organization who, thanks to Tori, we now know as The Syndicate, seem to have far more sinister intentions."

"Got it? Good. Now, any idea of how we track down this Dorian Granier character?" Dr. Connors asked.

Cayde raised his hand.

"What?" Dr. Connors asked. He was less than amused with Cayde at that moment.

"I have an idea."

"What is it? And it better not be anything stupid!" Christine said.

Dr. Connors gave Christine the sort of look a parent gives a child when they want them to mind their manners.

"Send Tori back in there and get Cooper to give us a location."

"He doesn't know anything else," Tori said.

Cayde did not believe that for a second. "Of course he does. He might not be high on the food chain within the Syndicate, but he isn't a scrub. He was specifically assigned with the task of making a statement. An organization as disciplined as the Syndicate seems to me wouldn't send some low level goon for such an assignment."

"He's got a point," James said.

"Wow, twice in one day someone's said you've got a point. That has to be a record," Christine said.

Cayde chuckled. "Stop it Christine. You're embarrassing yourself!" Cayde said with a flirtatious smile.

Christine glared at Cayde, which did nothing but amuse him.

"Knock it off you two. I agree with what Cayde said. Cooper has to know something. A contact number, a location, anything that will lead us to Dorian's whereabouts." Dr. Connors turned to his left to face Tori. "I want you to go back in there and get us a location."

"I'll try."

Dr. Connors glanced over to James who nodded in understanding. James followed Tori out of the room.

"Do you need more time to recuperate?" James asked once the two left the control room.

"No, I should be fine."

"Are you sure?"

Tori stopped in her tracks and thought for a second. "Yeah, I'm okay, I just want to get this over with as quickly as possible."

Tori opened the door and walked into the containment room. Cooper was on the ground shirtless doing pushups when she arrived. He stood up and stared at the two Ascendants. His initial reaction was to hit on the young woman, but after the pain she caused him earlier, he thought twice about it. "What do you want?"

"I want to know about Dorian Granier."

Cooper flinched ever so slightly. It was so subtle that Tori didn't even catch it, but James did.

"I don't know anyone by that name."

"He's lying," James said.

Tori moved forward and when she did, Cooper moved further away from the door that kept him locked in. Tori smiled slightly and was quite pleased with herself. It was nothing more satisfying to her than seeing a sleazebag like Cooper squirm. "You can either tell me what you know on your own or I can find out for myself. Either way, I'm going to get the information I need."

It took all James had within him to hide the way he felt in that moment. He had never been so proud of Tori as he was in that moment.

A worried look appeared on Cooper's face. "I don't know much about him."

"Tell us what you do know," Tori said.

Cooper was unsure of what to do. His eyes peered towards James for some sort of reaction, but James stood emotionless with his arms crossed.

"What do you want to know?"

"Whatever you know," Tori said.

Cooper glanced around nervously. He desperately tried to think of a way to get out of the predicament he found himself in. He tried to disintegrate the containment cell he was in, but the polytechnic adaptive materials kept him caged like a wild animal.

"You don't want to know Dorian Granier. In fact, you should forget that you ever heard the name. He is easily one of the most dangerous men you'll ever meet. Dorian Granier is proficient and extremely unpredictable. He's a professional, a master technician and extremely patient. I'd be willing to bet he's got a file on every single one of you and I guarantee his file is larger than anything you have on him."

"Is he the leader of the Syndicate?" James asked.

Cooper seemed almost surprised to hear James use the word Syndicate. Then again, he shouldn't have been, considering they used the name Dorian Granier.

"He asked you a question."

Cooper gave Tori the deadliest of stares. "I get that you're feeling all high and mighty now, but don't think for one second that you're tough." Tori did her best not to react.

"I promise you, the only thing keeping me from turning you and your bodyguard over there into a pile of ashes is this containment cell."

Cooper's threat put Tori back in her place. There was a lump in her throat as she processed what Cooper had said. Until that moment she felt in complete control. The rush she felt using her telepathy on him temporarily blinded her to the fact that Cooper was still extremely dangerous.

A slight smile flashed across Cooper's pale face and for a moment he felt as if he had regained control of the situation.

"Even if the containment field was down, you wouldn't be able to get passed either of us. Nice try with the intimidation factor, but neither of us are impressed," James said in an attempt to reestablish control.

Cooper's eyes turned back and forth between Tori and James before eventually settling in James direction. "I don't need telepathy to tell me how rattled she is. Like I said, she's nothing more than a little girl trying to play a grown man's game."

"Mr. Barrett, is Dorian Granier the leader of the Syndicate?" Tori asked. She stood as tall as she could to appear tough, but her small stature and lack of physical training betrayed her attempt.

"None of you understand the depth of my organization. If you truly believe that you Ascendants have what it takes to stop us, you are delusional. You would need an army to compete against us, and even then, it wouldn't be enough!"

James and Tori looked at one another. They both seemed hesitant as how to proceed. From the control room, Dr. Connors monitored the situation.

Dr. Connors was an extremely unique man as he held doctorate's degrees in both medicine and psychology. From monitoring Cooper, Dr. Connors could tell that he was stalling. "Tori, press him. He's hiding something," Dr. Connors said into her earpiece.

Tori did not respond to Dr. Connors, but she heard his instructions. The conversation was being monitored, and she didn't want Cooper to know. "Cooper, you and I both know that if you are hiding something, I will find it. I don't want to have to go digging in your head again, but I will. You know I will find the answers to the questions I seek, so please, just tell me and save yourself the headache."

Cooper stared at the young girl. He paced around the room and contemplated his options. Tori created a telepathic link with James to communicate with him without having to speak out loud.

"Do you think he'll give up his boss?" Tori asked telepathically.

"I'm not even sure he knows the answer to that. Especially if the Syndicate is as intricate as he claims," James replied in his head.

"Very well, I'll tell you what you want to know," Cooper suddenly said.

James and Tori broke the telepathic link they shared and turned their attention back to Cooper. James had a surprised look on his face. He hadn't expected Cooper to break so quickly.
"Go ahead, ask the question," Cooper said.

Tori hesitated. She peeked over to James for confirmation to proceed. James studied Cooper carefully. He squinted his eyes slightly as he tried to get a read on Cooper. Finally, James looked towards Tori and motioned for her to continue.
"Who is the leader of the Syndicate?"

"No, stop!" Dr. Connors shouted. His sudden yell startled everyone on the ship that was monitoring the exchange. His voice carried so loudly that it startled Tori and caused her to pull her earpiece out.

"Thank you," Cooper said with a smile. "The leader of the Syndicate is-"

Before Cooper to answer Tori's question, his eyes started to roll in the back of his head. Cooper fell to the ground and shook uncontrollably. He clutched at his head and withered in pain.

"What's happening?" Tori asked, eyes wide.

"I don't know," James replied.

A few seconds later Dr. Connors and Christine came rushing into the room. "Open the containment cell!" Dr. Connors ordered.

James rushed over to the panel and swiped his hand signature for confirmation. The cell opened and Dr. Connors hurried inside, but he was too late. By the time he reached Cooper, the Post Human had stopped moving. He laid on the ground lifeless.

Tori dropped to the ground and cried. "Did I do that?"

"No my dear, you didn't do that, the Syndicate did that." Dr. Connors replied. Dr. Connors looked over to Christine and James with heavy eyes. It was at that moment the Ascendants realized just how dangerous the Syndicate really was.

Chapter 4

A Face of Comfort

"Everyone settle down," Dr. Connors said. Cooper's death had the Ascendants on edge.

"He's dead isn't he? That man Tori was just interrogating suddenly died. How are we supposed to remain calm after that?" Tommy asked.

"Because we are professionals."

Tommy shook his head in disagreement. "That's where you're wrong. This is beyond our capabilities. We're dealing with professionals. We're dealing with an organization that's so far advance they can kill their operatives at the drop of a dime without even being nearby!"

"There's an explanation for this," a familiar voice said seemingly out of nowhere.

The group turned toward the voice and stared in confusion.

"Susan?" James said.

Susan Lee, Dr. Connors most trusted field member stood before the group with a serious look on her face. Her presence always brought comfort to the group. She had more field experience than all the Ascendants combined and could kick the behinds of just about any man.

"Susan, it's great to see you, but how did you get here so quickly?" Dr. Connors asked.

Suddenly a burst of air appeared in the spot right next to where Susan stood. When the air evaporated, a Chinese man stood right next to her. "Okay, just got word of a lead out in Shanghai," the man said to Susan.

"Do you need me to return?" Susan asked.

"No, that is not necessary. Thanks to your help we've hit the Triad with a devastating blow that will take them time to recover. We can take it from here, besides, looks like your team could really use your help."

Susan and the Chinese man shared a hug. When they finished their embrace, the man looked towards the group and nodded respectfully. "Take care of my sister and take care of yourselves."

"We will," Dr. Connors said with a slight head bow. Susan's brother nodded back and within the blink of an eye teleported off the ship and back to Shanghai.

"I don't get it, if he can just teleport anywhere he wants, why don't you have him teleport to the leader of the Triad's and take him out?"

"I'm sure there's a lot of things you don't get Cayde. Right now isn't the time to explain it though."

"What's going on Susan?" Dr. Connors asked in

a serious voice.

Susan looked over towards Christine. "I came as soon as I heard. Why didn't you tell me sooner what was happening?"

"You were busy. Helping your family deal with the Triad was just as important to anything we have going on here. I didn't want you distracted while you were in the field."

"I don't get distracted."

Cayde smiled. "Of course you don't, you're like a machine!"

Susan cracked a smile. It had been three months since she left the team to join her brother's mission against the Triad, and she had to admit that she had missed them.

"Ignore him!" Mia ran forward and gave Susan a big hug. Susan smiled back and embraced her fellow Ascendant. Even though the two women were ten years apart, surprisingly they had a lot in common and shared a sister-like bond.

"New haircut?"

Mia smiled and nodded.

"I like it," Susan said. She stepped back to check Mia out. "New haircut, new field outfit, you look leaner than ever, geez, it's like I've been gone for years."

Mia cheesed. If there was anyone's approval or validation she wanted, it was definitely Susan's. Susan had the sort of personality that was inspiring. Everyone in the group looked up to her and wanted her approval.

Susan looked around the room. "Dr. Connors, I should've been on that field mission and more importantly, I should've been involved with Cooper's interrogation."

Dr. Connors had a guilty look on his face. Like the rest of the group, he didn't like to disappoint her. "What's done is done. Tomorrow isn't guaranteed, so as dearly as you have been missed, it's good to know the group can function without you. Your training has turned them all into some very capable individuals."

Susan looked around the room at each member of the group. Whatever field skill they possessed was largely in part to her superior training. "All right, so from my understanding we've got a government agency whose motives we aren't too sure about and a criminal organization whose motives we are sure about. Does that pretty much sum things up?"

"Yes," Dr. Connors replied. Even though Dr. Connors is the leader of the Ascendants, there were many occasions where he took a step back to allow Susan to delegate directions. While Christine was probably one of the best analysts in the world, Susan was equally one of the best field operatives around. "This Commander Sullivan, I take it you know him?" Dr. Connors asked.

Susan nodded. "I served under him for seven years."

"What did you do?" Cayde asked.

"I served second in command under his special opts strike force unit."

"Strike force huh? You've must have really done a lot of killing to make a group like that," Cayde asked.

"Cayde!" Dr. Connors said.

"What, I'm just saying. Oh come on, you know there isn't a single person in here who isn't thinking the same thing. You have to be stone cold to be as effective as Susan."

"Let's just stay focus on the task at hand. If you're planning on confronting Commander Sullivan, I'm going with you," Susan said to Dr. Connors.

"Can he be trusted?"

"He's a secret agent. Of course not. You can't trust any of those guys. They all have agendas, and half the time, they aren't even really aware of what their own agenda is."

Dr. Connors scrunched his face. He was beginning to think like Tommy. Perhaps they were in over their head.

"If there's any chance that this Commander Sullivan character can be a potential ally, we have to take the risk."

"Umm, I think the chance of us being their allies

went out the window the moment we decided to intervene on their mission and capture Cooper," Cayde said.

Dr. Connors sighed.

"I mean what are you going to do? What are you going to say? Hey, we're really sorry about taking your capture, but we needed to ask him some questions. Oh yeah by the way, while we were questioning him, his head exploded, and now he's, you know, dead."

Dr. Connors looked about at nothing in particular for a moment before returning to address the group. He looked at Susan who was more than ready to do whatever needed to be done.

"Explaining what happened is exactly what we're going to do."

Cayde's eyes went big. "Wait what? I was only joking that's an absolutely terrible idea!"

"On the contrary. We head into this confrontation with this guy and hold back on intel, he'll see right through us. We have to be upfront and honest. That's the only chance we have at convincing this man we aren't the enemy."

"And what if we are? What if no matter what we say or do, they still view us as the enemy?" Cayde asked.

Dr. Connors thought for a moment. It was a question that he had pondered many times himself. From the moment the existence of Post Humans became public he wondered how the government would handle it. "We'll cross that bridge if the time ever comes."

Dr. Connors excused himself from the group and walked out of the room. Susan and Christine looked at one another and followed him back to his private office.

"You look worried," Susan said.

"I am, and I get the feeling there's something you aren't telling me."

Susan looked down and tried to avoid eye contact. Christine noticed the hesitation as did Dr. Connors. The silence made all three of them very uncomfortable.

"What is it Susan? I know how important that mission in China was to you. There's no way you would've left unless it was absolutely necessary. So what aren't you telling me?"

Susan looked around the room before finally locking eyes with Dr. Connors. "Towards the end of my tenure with Commander Sullivan, there was talk about another task force being formed. At the time I was serving under Julian Gunn and being prepped for my own command. They wanted me to lead this new task force."

"What sort of task force?" Christine asked.

"A task force to stop Post Humans."

Dr. Connors sighed. He had anticipated that being Susan's reply.

"Commander Sullivan said it was only a matter of time before the Post Human outbreak swept the nation and he wanted to be prepared. That's the thing with him. He's always two steps ahead of his opponent."

"That may be the case, but my fear is that he views us as the opponent and thus his eye isn't on the true evil," Dr. Connors said.

"The Syndicate," Christine said.

Dr. Connors nodded. "Exactly."

"Not to mention the sub group within the Syndicate," Christine said.

Susan looked at her funny. "What sub group?"

"Within the organization of the Syndicate is a specialized group of Post Humans known as the Chosen. Apparently they are responsible for gathering Post Humans to do their bidding."

Susan nodded in understanding. She had heard similar conversations being discussed in the past, but could never confirm the authenticity of the rumors. "So what's the plan?" Susan asked.

"Shortly, the ship will land and drop off Mia and James."

"Where are they going?" Susan asked.

"To pick up Lucas Morgan."

Susan made an uncomfortable sound with her mouth. "You really think going after Lucas is a good idea?"

"I think bringing Lucas in is a great idea.

Having his skill set backing us would greatly improve our situations in the field."

"I don't think he has any interest in returning to the group," Susan said.

"I believe he will. After learning more about this Syndicate, I think it's highly possible they took Lucas' sister Stephanie. He'll be interested in hearing that."

Susan still seemed uneasy about approaching Lucas, but she was willing to follow Dr. Connors orders.

"After we drop them off, the two of us and Cayde track Commander Sullivan down and see if we can come to an understanding," Dr. Connors said.

"Cayde?" Susan looked directly at Christine. "Why aren't you coming with us? You still haven't returned to the field?"

Christine swallowed spit. She did not want to have that conversation, especially not with Susan.

"She's not ready yet," Dr. Connors said.

Susan looked visibly upset. "What do you mean not ready? It's been a little over a year. What happened that day in the parking lot of your office wasn't your fault."

"It was my fault, I nearly killed that man."

"But you didn't and even had you of killed him, it wouldn't have been your fault. It's not as if you were aware of your own strength, it's not as if you set out to kill that man. You were defending yourself and in the process you discovered that you're one of the strongest people in the world."

"I wouldn't go that far."

Susan laughed. "I would. Anyone that can lift a truck off the ground is pretty strong to me." Christine nodded.

"Listen, if you aren't ready that's fine, whatever, but you better evaluate yourself. We need your abilities out in the field. I get that you're an excellent analyst, but there's going to come a time when we need your strength. There's going to come a time when we need your leadership and I must be certain that I can count on you. If I can't trust you, you're no good to me."

"Susan!" Dr. Connors said.

"It's okay sir, she's right."

Susan headed for the door. "Let me know when we're ready."

"Where are you going?" Dr. Connors asked.

"To change. If you want to meet Commander Sullivan, you need to be prepared for everything, and right now, I'm not prepared." Susan walked out of the room and headed back to her private quarters to get ready for a confrontation that could easily escalate.

"Are you okay?" Dr. Connors asked after Susan took her leave.

"Yeah, believe it or not, I appreciate Susan's

bluntness. She doesn't hold back. She pushes herself to the limit, and she expects the same level of commitment from those around her. I can't help but admire her."

"She is right when she said this isn't your fault. What happened was unfortunate, but it's because of situations like yours that we do what we do. These abilities are hard to understand and better yet, control. Not everyone that uses these abilities use them with the intention to harm and that's what we need to make certain Commander Sullivan understands," Dr. Connors said.

"Sir, we're landing," Tommy said.

"Understood. Is the tracker on Commander Sullivan still active?"

"Yes sir, I'm sending the coordinates to your phone as we speak."

Dr. Connors felt the left side of his pants vibrate. He reached inside his pocket and pulled out his cell phone.

"Where is he?" Christine asked.

"At the park," Dr. Connors said.

Christine raised an eyebrow. "That seems like an odd location for the head of a secret government agency to be."

"True, but let's be honest, we've seen odder things occur this past year."

Christine laughed. "Past year? Try past week."

The two shared a laugh. Christine followed Dr.

Connors out of his quarters and back into the control room.

"How are we looking?" Dr. Connors asked Tommy once everyone gathered back into the control room.

"We're ready to go whenever you are sir."

Dr. Connors glanced around the room. "I hope by the end of the day we'll be allies with this government agency. If for whatever reason something happens to us, Christine is in charge. You follow her lead as if it was mine."

Susan joined the group dressed for combat. She wore a sleek leather zip up body armor suit that housed a holster on her waist and a second holster by her leg.

Dr. Connors looked at her and chuckled with amusement. Here it was he had two men in his unit and it was the small Asian woman that was his fiercest warrior. He then turned his attention towards Mia and James. "You two be careful out there. Do what you can to bring Lucas in, but I don't want any unnecessary exposure on you guys."

"Don't worry sir, we'll take care of it," Mia said.

Dr. Connors nodded. He looked around the room again and beamed with pride. A year ago the group that stood before him were nothing more than runaways. Nothing more than a group of individuals seeking safety from a world that feared them. But now they were a team. Now they were a group of individuals determined to protect the Post Human race from those that would do it harm.

Dr. Connors looked towards Susan and Cayde. "You two ready?" They both nodded. "Alright, let's get this over with." Dr. Connors turned his attention to Christine. "Get the ship back here as soon as you can. Try to stay off the radar as much as possible."

"Sir, are you sure you don't want us to wait until the mission is over?"

Dr. Connors smiled. "Don't worry Christine, we'll be fine. Besides, with Susan here, I'm pretty sure they'll be the ones needing backup."

Dr. Connors, Susan and Cayde walked over to the hangar bay section of the ship and stood still. Christine waited until they were all in position and opened the door. Cayde closed his eyes and grimaced as the strong wind hit his face. "Tommy!"

"Yeah?"

"You need to work on some sort of beaming technology or something, because this skydiving thing we got going isn't going to work for me too much longer!"

"I'm working on it."

"Well, work faster!" Cayde shouted and with that said, he jumped out of the plane, followed by Susan and Dr. Connors. "Have I ever told you guys I'm ridiculously afraid of heights?"

"What?" Dr. Connors shouted. The strong wind that blew made it very difficult for Dr. Connors to hear anything that was said.

"I said-"

"Stop talking Cayde, concentrate on landing safely!" Susan shouted. Susan put her hands by her side and positioned herself in a form that resembled a human missile. She shot down to the ground and pulled on the cord. Susan was the first to land, and she did so perfectly. Dr. Connors was next, he too landed with no trouble. The two looked up into the sky and noticed Cayde struggle to get the cord pulled. "What is he doing?" Susan asked.

"Something's wrong with his cord. Cayde can you hear me?" Dr. Connors got no answer. "Cayde? Do you hear me?" Cayde descended with increased velocity. "He's not going to make it!"

Dr. Connor's face was paler than normal as he watched Cayde plummeted. He watched in horror as Cayde struggled to get his shoot to open. Finally, after several attempts, Cayde was able to pull on his cord and get the shoot to open. He came in far too hot and as a result, hit the ground hard. He rolled several times before coming to a stop.

Dr. Connors and Susan rushed over to check on his status. "Cayde!" Dr. Connors called out, but received no answer. Susan easily outran Dr. Connors and reached Cayde first. Cayde laid face down and there was no sign of movement.

"Cayde!" Susan said. She rolled Cayde over and to her surprise, he had a big smile on his face. Slowly, Cayde made it to his feet.

"Oh, thank God!" Dr. Connors said when he made it to them and saw that Cayde was still alive.

"That's it, as soon as this meeting is over, we're getting some sort of beaming technology on the ship. I am far too valuable to be rolling around on the ground!"

Dr. Connors and Susan looked at one another. They shook their head at Cayde's comment.

"Where the heck are we?" Cayde asked.

"Someone's backyard about a block away from the park," Susan replied.

"Umm, wouldn't it make more sense to land near the location where we're meeting this guy?"

"No, not when we're trying to hold on to the element of surprise," Susan said.

Cayde wiped off the dirt on his shirt and shook his head. "Well, I'll forgo the whole element of surprise factor if it means there's less walking involved."

Susan shook her head. "You of all people have no reason to complain when it comes to transportation!"

Cayde laughed. "Yeah, you've got a point!"

"Who are you?" a smile little voice said from behind them.

Dr. Connors, Susan and Cayde all turned around at the same time to face the voice. "Well hello there, I'm Cayde, who are you?" Cayde stuck out his hand and held it in front of him.

The little girl looked at him cautiously and moved back. "My mommy says I'm not supposed to talk to strangers."

Cayde rescinded his hand and took a step back away from the little girl. "Your mommy is absolutely correct. We were just leaving now. You take care."

Cayde turned his back to the little girl and moved with a hastened pace. Dr. Connors and Susan waved goodbye to her and followed behind closely.

The little girl watched the three leave. She had no idea that they were on a mission to save her future and that of thousands, possibly millions more like her.

Chapter 5

A Meeting of Two Heads

"How much further?" Cayde asked.

Dr. Connors looked down at his cell phone and tracked the small blue dot indicating the commander's position. "Right over there."
Dr. Connors, Susan and Cayde looked forward and saw a large burly man sitting on a bench reading a newspaper.

"Is that him?" Cayde asked.

"Yes, that's him," Susan replied hesitantly.

"You sound nervous," Cayde said.

"If you think I'm dangerous, just consider for a second that this is the man that trained me."

Cayde stood still with his mouth wide open. "Yeah, that's a good point. Maybe we should rethink this plan."

As the three approached Cayde couldn't help but notice the massive size the man possessed.

"The park is empty. Less chance for any casualties if this meeting doesn't go well," Dr. Connors said. That didn't bring much comfort to Cayde.

"He isn't alone," Susan whispered.

Dr. Connors stopped his approach. "What do you mean?"

"The man standing near the other bench. He's one of the commander's men. Commander Sullivan is on to us."

Dr. Connors casually turned his attention to the other man. He noticed the space Commander Sullivan had, but yet at the same time, the other man was well within striking distance if need be. "This other guy, did you work with him?"

Susan paused. "Yeah, I worked directly under him. He was the first in command under the task force I worked with."

Dr. Connors and Cayde stopped in their tracks. They both turned to face Susan.

"Yeah that's it, I'm calling it, this mission is officially screwed. We need to turn back around and get out of here before it's too late," Cayde said.

"The ship is gone, we are going to complete our mission," Dr. Connors said.

Cayde shook his head uncomfortably. "I don't like this, what purpose would an agent like that have at the park? This is starting to smell like a set up!"

Susan was about to say something in reply but she stopped when she heard Commander Sullivan's slow rhythmic clap. "Good for you Mr. Brady, I was wondering if there was more to you than just comic relief. I'm glad to see you have some wits about you," Commander Sullivan said.

Dr. Connors and the two Ascendants took up a defensive position.

"Oh please, I saw you three coming miles away... Literally. Obviously you guys went through a lot of trouble to get to me, so I'm curious to hear what's on your mind. Come, join me."

Susan and Cayde followed close behind Dr. Connors. They stood guard while he took a seat on the same bench as Commander Sullivan.

"Dr. Connors. A doctor of medicine and psychology. One of the biggest philanthropist in the lovely state of Washington and also one of the richest in town. Quite the resume, did I miss anything?"

"Yes, I'm also the leader of the Ascendants." Commander Sullivan removed his sunglasses and gave Dr. Connors an amused stare. Susan shifted on the balls of her feet while across from her Special Agent Julian Gunn did the same.

"Now we're getting somewhere. You call yourselves the Ascendants. Interesting choice for a name."

"We are here to make sure that the lives of the Post Human population are protected."

Commander Sullivan studied Dr. Connors carefully. He found the man to be quite intriguing and saw an opportunity to play a game of chess.

"Protect them how? What exactly are your intentions? Do you plan on protecting those that break the law as well?"

"Absolutely not."

Commander Sullivan turned his head and motioned for Special Agent Julian Gunn. Julian nodded and approached his commanding officer. He handed Commander Sullivan a tablet, and locked eyes momentarily with Susan before taking a step back.

"I was very curious to see how you answered my question about protecting the Post Humans that break the law. I can see that you have two different operatives with you this time, but I believe these individuals here on this video are part of your group as well." Commander Sullivan handed Dr. Connors the tablet and pressed play. The video of Mia and James interference with Commander Sullivan's task force played. "So I'm curious, how do you explain this?"

Dr. Connors turned off the video and handed the tablet back to the commander. "The individual responsible for the attack was named Cooper Barrett. We do not condone his actions at all."

"And yet when my men tried to detain him, your group just happened to be there to extract him."

Dr. Connors smiled slightly to keep his composure. He knew the commander was trying to play mind games, and he knew exactly how to handle him.

"Regardless if you like the Post Human race or not. The fact remains that they have rights. Rights that we, the Ascendants, will not let be violated."

"Violated? What rights of Mr. Barrett's were violated? It was a pretty standard mission until that girl of yours came along and made my agent's weapons float in the air."

Commander Sullivan looked over to Julian to see if indeed any of his men had violated Cooper's rights.

"In the past month, seven Post Humans have turned up dead. Six of the seven were murdered and the death of the other one was ruled a suicide, but I have my doubts about that as well."

Commander Sullivan swiped left to unlock his tablet and flipped through files. He typed in his passcode to access the files and handed the tablet over to Dr. Connors. "Are these the individuals you speak of?"

Dr. Connors took a glance at the files and nodded in confirmation. "Now, I don't know much about any of these individuals on this file, but they were people, and they deserved better than to be murdered simply because they were different. Heck, even if they committed a crime, they still deserved a trial. They didn't deserve to have their life taken away, regardless of how much of a risk you believe them to be."

"Oh I agree, the presence of Post Humans is indeed a major threat to national security, but the individuals on these files did not die at the hands of myself or any of my agents. We assumed you were responsible for their deaths."

Dr. Connors kept his cool but his head spun with multiple theories on if the Commander was deflecting blame or was actually sincere. "Why would we kill our own?"

"Ever been to Chicago? They kill each other every day like it's some kind of sport or video game. I don't know why, perhaps they wanted to expose you and you decided to shut them up permanently. Perhaps they were weak and didn't fit your vision of what Ascendants should be. I don't know, all I know is that there are a bunch of dead bodies, and the only organization I can think of responsible for this is you."

Silence filled the air. Dr. Connors wanted to let the commander's words sink in. He wanted to take a second to frame his next words carefully. These sort of meetings were all about being able to make your case.

"Commander Sullivan, we recently had the opportunity to interrogate Cooper Barrett, and we found out some interesting things."

Commander Sullivan shook his head in annoyance. "See that right there is a problem to me.

What gives you the right to interrogate anyone? You aren't law enforcement. You took a man that we had every right to capture and you denied us the opportunity to get information from him."

Commander Sullivan looked around the park. "Where is he by the way? He's a criminal, and he has to pay for his crimes. The judicial system will handle him, not you guys."

Dr. Connors looked towards Susan. He knew he was in a tough spot and things were only going to get tougher.

"Well, where is he?"

"He's dead," Dr. Connors replied confidently.

Cayde shook his head. "Yeah, that doesn't make us look very good."

"Shut it Cayde," Susan hissed. Cayde quickly obliged.

Commander Sullivan raised an eyebrow and gave Dr. Connors a hard look. "He's dead? So just hours after you interfere in our operation, the man we needed intel from ends up dead? That's pretty convenient, wouldn't you say?"

"Not convenient at all actually. We had more questions for him."

Commander Sullivan stood up. His movement immediately prompted Susan to shift her stance, which in turn caused Julian Gunn to do the same. Cayde stood around nervously. He had this funny feeling that things weren't going to end well for them and he was ready to get his group out of harm's way.

"So how did Mr. Barrett die?" Commander Sullivan asked.

Dr. Connors hesitated slightly. He wasn't quite sure how to explain what happened.

"He had perhaps an aneurism or something like that. One moment he was talking and then the next he was on the ground in pain," Cayde said.

Commander Sullivan did not acknowledge Cayde at all. He kept his eyes locked on Dr. Connors and waited for the doctor's reply.

"Mr. Brady over there is correct, although his words could've been articulated a bit better. Mr. Barrett was about to reveal crucial information to us when suddenly he experienced an excruciatingly painful sensation which caused trauma to the brain. He died instantly."

"What sort of crucial information was he about to reveal?"

"The leader of a massive criminal organization known as the Syndicate."

Julian Gunn's ears perked up when he heard the name. He moved swiftly and stood next to his commander. Susan followed suite and moved next to Dr. Connors.

"Oh man, it's about to go down!" Cayde said. Cayde stood on the left side of Dr. Connors, and did his best to hide the concern on his face, but both of the agents could easily see passed it.

"Cooper Barrett mentioned the Syndicate to you?" Agent Gunn asked.

Susan seemed surprised by Julian's demeanor. She knew him well enough to know if he was asking questions, there was something important on his mind. "Yes, Cooper stated that he was indeed a member of the Syndicate. We pulled up surveillance of Mr. Barrett and found multiple images of him with a guy named Dorian Granier. We believe Dorian Granier to be a top player within the Syndicate's organization."

Commander Sullivan and Agent Gunn had a concern look on their face. They took several steps away from the Ascendants and conversed with one another.

"I have a bad feeling about this. I think maybe we should leave before things get any tenser," Cayde said.

"We're fine," Dr. Connors said.

"I agree, the words Syndicate and Dorian Granier caused a pretty strong reaction from them." Susan studied her former colleagues carefully. She didn't know exactly what they were thinking, but she knew they were concerned. Which at the very least meant they believed some of what Dr. Connors had to say.

After a lengthy conversation, Commander Sullivan and Special Agent Gunn made their way back towards Dr. Connors and company. The Ascendants were on edge as they watched the muscle defined men move towards them.

"We're going to need to bring you three in for further questioning," Commander Sullivan said.

Cayde gritted his teeth. "I told you, I knew these guys were going to pull some crap like this. I'm not going, there's no way I'm going anywhere with you guys!"

Commander Sullivan cocked his head slightly. "Mr. Brady, don't make a scene. So far this meeting has been far more cordial than I anticipated. Don't ruin it now."

"Then don't come near me."

"Cayde, calm down, we're all okay here," Dr. Connors said.

Special Agent Gunn stepped forward and moved towards Cayde. Cayde took a step back and warned the agent not to move any closer, but the agent completely disregarded Cayde's warning. Susan moved to her left and occupied the space between Special Agent Gunn and Cayde. "That's far enough Julian."

"Former agent Susan Lee, it's been a while."

"Not long enough," Susan replied.

"It was nothing personal, I was simply following orders."

Susan glared at Julian. "Following orders? We were partners, and you betrayed me."

"I didn't betray you, I followed my orders. I was told to bring you in and that's exactly what I did." Susan smirked. "You mean that's exactly what you tried to do, because as you can see, clearly you didn't bring me in back then and you aren't going to do it now either."

Cayde swallowed spit. The moment he feared seemed to be inching dangerously close to becoming a reality.

"Susan you know good and well I felt sorry for you. I held back that day and you know it. But that sympathy I had for you, whatever sense of loyalty I felt for you and the situation you were in is over. You're coming back with us. Now you can make things easy or you can be difficult about it. The choice is yours."

Julian clenched his fists and prepared himself. He knew the sort of character Susan possessed and knew that the easy way just wasn't in her DNA.

"Susan, remember what we came here for," Dr. Connors said.

"I do, but more importantly, I remember what our purpose is."

Without hesitation, Susan jumped off the ground, brought both her legs to her abdomen and leveled Julian with a front donkey kick to his chest. Most men would've fell flat on their backs, but not Julian. While falling, Julian quickly contorted his body and did a side somersault flip to regain his balance. In a fluid motion, Julian turned back around and took up a defensive position just as Susan followed up with another attack.

"Shame, we almost made it without incident," Commander Sullivan said to Dr. Connors.

"We still can Commander, call your agent off."

"Too late for that, besides, those two need to hash out their differences." Commander Sullivan turned his back on the doctor and began to walk away.

Susan aggressively swung with a closed fist right-hand punch aimed for Julian's face. This time Julian was ready. He brought his hands up in an X motion and blocked the attack.

He countered, grabbed Susan's arm, swiftly twirled behind her and locked his hands around her waist. He attempted to use a belly to back wrestling move on her, but Susan broke free of the hold and nailed Julian with an elbow to the face.

"I'm better than you," Susan said.

"You're good Susan, you're really good, but you aren't better than me."

Julian ran hard directly at Susan. He started to move to his left, but in mid stride he pivoted and changed directions. Julian left the ground, twirled his body in the air and kicked Susan in the side of the face.

Susan fell to the ground but quickly recovered. She got back to her feet and anxiously waited for

Julian to make another move. Julian started forward, but had to change course when he saw Cayde approach from the corner of his eye. Julian swung, but Cayde moved faster than Julian could see. In the blink of an eye Cayde went from Julian's left side to his right side. He hit Julian with a flurry of punches with seemed to have minimal impact at best.

"A speedster, so that's your contribution to the team. Okay, good to know," Julian said.
Cayde went for another attack, but Julian caught Cayde's left arm before he could connect. Julian nailed Cayde with an elbow to the abdomen and followed up with a closed fist to the face.

Cayde stumbled backwards and fell to the ground. He slowly made his way back to his feet and hesitantly took up a defensive position.

"Cayde, I've got it. Get Dr. Connors out of here!"

Cayde looked at Susan with defiance.

"Now Cayde!"

Begrudgingly, Cayde left the fight and ran over to check on Dr. Connors.

"You always were a good partner. He doesn't even realize that you just saved his life," Julian said.

"Perhaps I just saved yours."

Julian laughed. "Oh please, he might be fast, but he's no match for me. You know as well as I do that punk isn't even in the same league as me."

Susan knew what Julian said to be true, but there was no way she was about to give him that bit of satisfaction.

"Come on Susan, what are we doing here? I don't want to fight you, even more so, I don't want to hurt you."

"How did you think this was going to go? We aren't about to be subjected to any of the interrogation tactics you all have planned. I was with you guys for years, I know how this goes. I won't let you do to Dr. Connors and Cayde what we did to those we captured for all those years."

Susan kept her defensive stance as did Julian. The two danced around one another while they tried to figure out their next move.

"You know I can't let you leave, not this time," Julian said.

"Then you better stop me, because leave is exactly what I'm going to do."

Susan ran forward and caught Julian by the head with her legs. She pushed forward and released her grip in midair. Julian went flying but managed to land on his feet. He gritted his teeth and stared hard at his former protégé.

"The Syndicate, did Dr. Connors mean what he said about them?"

Susan, who was about to advance once more stopped and let her guard down slightly.

"Yes, he meant every word. They are the real threat

out there not us. I don't know what all your organization is about, but if you want to protect the public, it's the Syndicate you need to focus on."

"Dorian Granier, do you really know where he is?" Julian asked.

Susan was about to answer Julian but before she could, the sound of gunfire bellowed through the park. A single bullet was fired, and it lodged itself right between Susan's eyes.

"Susan!" Julian shouted. Julian jumped on top of Susan to shield her from another attack. He looked around the area for the shooter but saw no signs of one.

Cayde, who had just finished getting Dr. Connors out of harm's way returned to the scene just in time to see Susan fall to the ground.

"Susan!" he shouted. Cayde sped over and attempted to punch Julian, but Julian caught Cayde's fist and showed mercy on him. Julian simply pushed Cayde backwards instead of seriously hurting him.

"Don't test me Cayde." Julian's eyes seemed to penetrate through Cayde's soul. The young man did not want to test Julian and smartly backed away.

"Julian, let's move!" Commander Sullivan shouted. Julian gritted his teeth as he took one last look at Susan's lifeless body.

"I'll find whoever did this and make them pay!"

Julian said to Cayde. Julian kept low and made his way down to the end of the street where an unmarked SUV waited for him.

A tear fell from Cayde's face as he gently lifted Susan's body off the ground. He looked high and low for the shooter but saw no sign of one. Defeated, Cayde placed Susan's body over his shoulder and sped out of harm's way.

Chapter 6

Unwanted Encounters

"We're entering visibility Tommy, how's the cloak coming along?" Christine asked through her earpiece.

"Enabling cloak in 3,2,1." Tommy locked the cloaking device into place and watched as it turned and positioned itself comfortably in its slot. It took about five seconds, but the cloaking device activated and was ready to be used. "We're good to go Christine."

"Roger that, landing in the parking lot now." Christine eased off the throttle and guided the ship down gently. She had become a bit of a pro at piloting. She was easily the best pilot of the group. Dr. Connors and James were the only others in the group that had flown the ship. Tommy had developed a pretty advanced autopilot system in the event that there was no one available to fly the plane, but he hoped he'd never have to use it.

"What time is it?" James asked.

"12:45 which means we have about fifteen minutes before Lucas' lunch break is over," Mia said.

James stared at her.

"What?" Mia asked.

James shook his head. "Nothing."

Mia stepped in front of James and placed her hand on his massive chest. Seeing the two so close to one another really displayed the ginormous difference in size between them. Mia looked like a small child compared to James' tall and muscular stature. Nevertheless, with Mia's telekinesis and training from Susan, not even James wanted to mess with her.

"It's something, spill it."

"I'm just trying to decide if this is a good idea or not."

"Decide if what's a good idea?"

James looked at her as if she should know the answer to her own question, but she pretended as if she didn't. "You know good and well what I'm talking about Mia. You know the man's lunch schedule. How much more obvious can you be?"

Mia shook off the subtle accusation. "I know his lunch schedule because I talked to him for a few minutes last week. It's a detail, and Susan's been training me to pay close attention to all details. No matter how big or small they seem."

"Mhm, whatever you say Mia."

"Oh, whatever James!" Mia rolled her eyes and looked around the hangar bay room. She noticed an empty water bottle and smiled mischievously. Mia flicked her left hand forward and sent the water bottle flying in James' direction. The playful attack caught James by surprise and hit him in the side of the head.

"Really Mia? Real mature!" James shook off the bottle attack and focused his attention to the outside. He looked to see if the coast was clear and when he was confident it was, he had Christine open the hangar bay doors.

"Alright, let's do this," Mia said. She strutted passed James and made her way to the sidewalk.

"Hey, you want to slow down a bit?" James said.

Mia huffed. "With those long legs of yours, you should have no reason not to be able to keep up."

"You know Mia; you can be a real brat at times!"

Mia flashed her gorgeous smile and batted her long eyelashes. "Maybe, but you still love me anyway."

"Yeah, yeah, let's just get this over with. It's been a long day already."

"Yeah, it has. How do you think things went with Dr. Connors?"

"I'm sure everything went okay," James said as he used his long strides to catch up to Mia. The two approached the front door at the same time. Mia tried to open the door, but it was locked.
"Attention to detail huh?"

"What?"

James pointed to the small circular gray button that rested on the right side of the brick wall. "You have to be buzzed in silly."

"Oh yeah, I saw it." Mia did her best to play the oversight off. "The school has a no guns allowed sign right here. You probably should've left your side arm on the plane."

"Yeah, I don't think so. I don't like to take any chances."

The secretary buzzed the two Ascendants inside the building.

"Let me do all the talking," Mia said. She stepped forward and waited for the secretary to buzz her inside the junior high office.

"Hi, can I help you?" the secretary asked.

"Umm yes, we're here to see Mr. Morgan."

"Is he expecting you?"

"No he isn't, we wanted it to be a surprise."

"I see, and you two are?"

Mia and James looked at one another as if they shared a telepathic link, but unfortunately the link only worked when Tori was around to establish a connection. "I'm his sister Mia and this is his best friend James."

A bright smile appeared on the secretary's face. "Oh, well that's wonderful, I'm sure Mr. Morgan will be delighted to see you two! I just need you guys to sign in really quick for me."

"Delighted to see us isn't the word I would use," James mumbled.

Mia stepped a bit closer to James and stepped on his toe. James grimaced slightly and smiled through the pain. He glared at Mia, but she refused to meet his stare. James and Mia finished signing in and waited patiently for the secretary to give them visitor passes. She instructed them on how to reach the teacher's lounge and sent them on their way.

"You think we should've used fake names?" Mia asked.

"Oh now you're worried about giving out your real name?"

"I'm serious, after today, that government organization is going to be looking for us."

"Well it's too late now. They already know our names thanks to you."

Mia rolled her eyes. "Let it go James, I'm not that used to going up against potentially hostile government agencies."

"Yeah, that much is clear."

As the two passed the first hall, and made their way up the stairs, Mia noticed a stapler lying on the ground. She looked at the stapler and then at James and smiled.

"Don't even think about it," James said in a deep voice.

"I have no idea what you are talking about." Mia batted her eyes playfully and pretended to look all innocent. It was an act she intended James not to fall for.

"There." James pointed to the room with the red door on the right-hand side of the hall. "This must be it."

Mia concurred. She fought back the smile that formed on the edge of her mouth, took a deep breath and walked inside. James followed closely behind her.

So I walk down to the elementary side of the building and I head on over to Ms. Marquette's room. Jimmy sees me and immediately runs up to me. He looks at me, smiles and says I like you, you're a good man. So I smile back and I say thanks Jimmy you're a good boy. He laughs and says yeah I know," Lucas Morgan said to his fellow coworker Samantha Meyers.

Samantha laughed emphatically. "These kids are absolutely adorable." Her laughter quickly turned to curiosity when she realized that Lucas was no longer laughing with her.

"Mia, James, what are you doing here?" Lucas asked. His reception for the two was less than warm.

"Hey Lucas," Mia said with a wide smile.

"Well hello there," Samantha said. She completely disregarded Mia and focused all her attention on James. She gave her best seductive smile as she stared at the handsome man. "Lucas, aren't you going to introduce me to your friends?"

Lucas did his best to hide his anger, but Mia and James could see pass the facade.

"Hi, my name is Mia, Lucas' sister, and this is James, Lucas' best friend." Mia extended her hand for Samantha to shake. Samantha had a perplex look on her face. She had come to know Lucas pretty well and not once had he mentioned a sister or a best friend in any of their conversations.

"Hi, I'm Samantha Meyer. Fifth grade science teacher." Samantha gave Mia a respectful smile before moving passed her to greet James. Samantha extended her hand to James which he politely shook. She wore a big smile on her face as she stared into James' dark brown eyes. She let her hand linger in his just a tad bit longer than most do on greetings. James could sense her attraction to him, and had it been any other day, he probably would've explored the possibilities.

"Hi Samantha, it's nice to meet you," Mia said before turning back to Lucas. "Surprise."

Lucas was less than amused. "Mia, what are you doing here?"

"Lucas, you've been holding out on me. You never told me you had a sister, and you definitely didn't tell me you were friends with such a handsome man."

James smiled and thanked Samantha for the compliment. Mia, who had witnessed a similar stare from a number of women directed towards James rolled her eyes. Sure, she couldn't deny herself that James was quite pleasing to look at, but the way some of these women threw themselves at him made her sick.

"Yeah, somehow throughout all the conversations we've had, it must have slipped my mind," Lucas said.

Due to the secret life he lived, he had no choice but to go along with Mia's lie.

Samantha looked up at the clock and frowned. Her break was over and she needed to get back to her class, but she found herself wanting to stick around James just a bit longer.

"Well it was really nice meeting you," Samantha said to Mia.

"Yeah, you too," Mia replied.

Samantha moved closer to James and shook his hand again. "Don't be a stranger, come by more often!"

"Yeah, I'll definitely try," James said.

Hesitantly, Samantha headed for the door and left the three Post Humans alone.

"Are you two out of your mind?" Lucas hissed quietly. His face was red, and it took everything within him not to yell.

"We need your help," Mia said.

Lucas shook his head and gestured that he wanted no part in anything they were up to. "You guys need to leave, I've really made a life for myself here and I don't need you two screwing things up for me."

"Really? Screwing things up for you, is that what you think of when you think of me?" the tone in Mia's voice indicated that she was hurt by Lucas' words.

"Don't do that, don't stand there and try to make me feel bad for leaving," Lucas said. His attention shifted back and forth between the two.

"Oh don't look at me, I don't care at all that you left. I've said from the start we didn't need you around."

"Right, you discover you've got incredible strength and now all of a sudden you're a tough guy."

James laughed. "Long before I ever developed these abilities I was a tough guy. Playing college football, doing construction work, being a bouncer. These abilities simply enhanced an already developed muscle."

"Yeah whatever man. Look, I respect what Dr. Connors is trying to accomplish with you guys and I wish you all the best of luck, but I can't be dragged back into that world. Call me selfish, call me scared, but the climate between Humans and Post Humans is heating up, and I want no part of it. I just want to live a normal life. I just want to live a peaceful life and give these children the gift of knowledge."

"That's the whole point Lucas, nothing will be peaceful if we don't make a stand," Mia said.

Lucas shook his head. "You see, I bet you a lot of these radical groups and terrorist groups started out simple like you guys and over time they became more and more fanatic with their mission. You guys are creating an army of Post Humans. You're playing with fire and it's just a matter of time before that fire ignites, and when it does, I don't want to be anywhere near it." Lucas grabbed his containers and placed it back in his lunch bag. He proceeded to throw out his trash and waited for James and Mia to leave.

"Lucas?"

"I mean it Mia; you need to leave. There's nothing you can say or do that's going to make me come with you. You guys have your agenda and I respect that, but now I need you to respect the fact that I have no interest in returning."

Lucas headed for the door but James stood in front of it and refused to move. "Really man, you want to go this route with me?" Lucas asked.

"I don't want to, but I'm not letting you leave, not until Mia is done talking."

Lucas chuckled. "That's right, you're her bodyguard or something correct? Tell me, how does it feel knowing someone half your size could take you out with the simplest of ease?"

James gave a fake smile and before Lucas could react, James lifted Lucas off the ground by the throat and held him in place. Lucas tried to free himself from James' clutches, but he struggled to break free. James tossed him in the air like a sack of potatoes. Lucas landed awkwardly on the couch inside the teacher's lounge. "No enhanced strength needed to kick your behind. You really don't want this fight Lucas."

Lucas hopped off the couch quickly and ran straight for James. He attempted to hit James with a right cross, but James ducked low and tackled Lucas right back into the couch. James was about to follow up his attack with a punch to the face, but an invisible force held his arm in place. Lucas took advantage of the situation and kicked James off of him.

Both men got back to their feet and attempted another attack, but Mia intervened and sent both men flying in opposite directions with the use of her telekinesis.

"Enough! I didn't come here to see the two of you fight."

James and Lucas huffed. They both wanted to go another round, but they were certain Mia wouldn't allow it. She had her telekinesis in such control that neither men would have a chance against her if she really wanted to stop them.

"So is this your plan, intimidate people like me

until we do what you want?"

"Don't be ridiculous Lucas, you know it isn't like that."

"Really? Because as far as I'm concerned, that's exactly what it's like. Here I was minding my own business, enjoying my day, when suddenly two uninvited guests show up. Two uninvited guests that have made it their mission to try and get me to do something I want no part in."

James grunted. In that moment he wanted nothing more than to use his strength on Lucas, but Mia's interest in Lucas caused James to refrain from such actions.

"The reason that we are here more so than anything else is to find out about Dorian Granier," Mia said.

Lucas gave Mia a worried look. "Dorian Granier? Why would you mention that name to me?"

Mia and James looked at one another. "I read your file, I know that a little over a year ago you and your brother were captured by an unknown group of scientists."

Mia immediately regretted bringing up Lucas' past. It wasn't something he wanted to talk about. "We have reason to believe that this organization that experimented on you and others like us is an organization known as the Syndicate. We don't know much about them, but we were able to identify an individual we suspect to be a high ranking member within the organization."

Lucas studied Mia hard. "And you believe this Dorian Granier person is someone that I know?"

"I believe he's someone you might have heard of, or now that we know this organization is the same organization that captured you and your brother, there might be something that you can tell us that will help us find out more about them."

"I don't know anything about them and even if I did, these aren't the type of people you want to mess with. Now if you will excuse me, my lunch break is over."

James cracked his knuckles and moved closer towards Lucas. Mia used her telekinesis to hold James in place.

"Come on Lucas, don't be like that. You must know something."

Lucas shook his head. "I don't know anything about this organization you're talking about. All I know is that my brother, and I were captured by some man and knocked unconscious. When I came to, I was in some facility being rescued by a group of black opts soldiers or something."

Mia and James looked at one another.

"This man, what did he look like?" James asked.

"I don't remember; it was over a year ago."

James gritted his teeth. "Try anyway."

Lucas huffed. He relaxed his defensive stance

and thought back to his time in the facility. He tried to replay the details of that horrible time, but a lot of it was still fuzzy.

"Please Lucas, anything you can tell us would be great."

"I don't remember."

James shook his head. He did not believe Lucas for one moment. "This was probably one of the worst days of your life Lucas. You don't just forget about something like that."

"If I remembered anything I would tell you. Especially if it meant I could finally be rid of you two."

"You don't mean that," Mia said.

Lucas looked directly at Mia. "Yeah, I kind of do."

Mia looked over to James. "He might be suppressing his memory. It was after all a traumatic event."

"Well, if that's the case, we need to get him back to the ship and let Tori read his mind. She should be able to recover any suppressed memories he might have. If not, she can easily read his thoughts and uncover whatever it is he's hiding." James gave Lucas a hard look, a look that made it clear that he didn't believe Lucas.

"I'm not going back anywhere with you two. Now I'm only going to say this one more time before things turn really ugly."

Lucas did not have time to follow through on his threat. The confrontation between the three Post Humans was interrupted by the sounds of screams coming from the hallway. Lucas glared at James and Mia. They looked at one another unsure of what the commotion was about.

"Stay here," James said.

James pulled out his gun, opened the door and calmly walked out into the hallway.

"Everywhere you guys go, trouble follows. I have no idea what's causing the screaming, but I bet you had something to do with it!"

Mia had no words to say. Each dig Lucas made cut deeper and deeper into her.

"What is it with you two anyway?" Lucas asked.

"What are you talking about?"

Lucas had an offended look on his face. He didn't consider for one second that Mia didn't know what he was talking about. "You and James."

"Lucas, he's my partner, and a really good friend. We're in the field a lot together, which means we spend a lot of our time with each other. Plus, I genuinely enjoy his company."

"How could you enjoy the company of a guy who's nothing more than a hothead?"

Mia stretched her hands forward and knocked Lucas back down to the couch. "James is one of the kindest, smartest men I know. There's so much more to him than you realize. Just like there's so much more to you than he realizes. You two just seem to bring out the worse in one another."

Before Lucas could reply, James returned and looked completely terrified. "You two are going to want to come out here." James paused. "Well, I take that back, you probably don't want to come out here, but come out here anyway!"

Mia and Lucas looked at one another with worried expressions. Lucas got back off the couch and followed James and Mia out of the room. Lucas' jaw dropped, and he nearly threw up his lunch as he stared at Samantha's lifeless body. "What happened?" Mia asked James.

Several panicked teachers ran passed the three and didn't bother to look back. "That happened," James said. He pointed down to the end of the hall.

"I don't see anything. What am I looking for?" Mia asked.

James kept his finger pointed down the hall. "Wait for it!" Suddenly something massively well-built and tall emerged from around the corner of the other hall. It had skin the color of blood, long black dreadlocks that were tied at the top, and tribal tattoos on its face.

"What in the world is that?" Lucas asked.

"I have no idea," Mia said.

Lucas looked back over at his now deceased coworker Samantha. She had a large hole that went straight through her body. It looked as if some sort of extremely powerful and hot weapon was used to cause such a deadly result.

"Guess there's no need to ask if it's friendly or not."

James reached to his left leg and pulled out his secondary firearm. "Now you see why I never enter the field without my gun. Doesn't matter what the mission is, I ain't taking any chances."

"Agreed."

James took a step forward and was about to fire on the hostile, but he froze when he saw the aggressive being snatch up a woman like she was nothing. The hostile seemed to examine her. He looked her up and down and sniffed her as if she was a piece of meat. It must've been dissatisfied, because after a quick examination, it snapped the woman's neck like a twig and tossed her aside.

"Oh God!" Mia shouted. Her entire body jerked back at the sight.

"Okay buddy, that's enough," James said angrily. James squared his feet, pulled the trigger of both guns and fired until the clip was empty. The bullets bounced off the hostile like it was nothing.

"I think you're just making him angrier," Lucas said.

"Yeah, no kidding," James replied.

"What kind of Post Human looks like that?" Mia asked.

James looked the hostile over. "I don't think it's a Post Human at all." James, Mia and Lucas shared a look that needed no words. They all were thinking the same thing and in that moment the thought of what the hostile represented made the situation as dire as it was with the Syndicate seem trivial.

The hostile dusted itself off and found the bullets to be nothing more than a minor inconvenience. It studied the three Post Humans carefully and decided to counter James attack. The hostile reached behind his back and pulled out a long weapon that looked similar to a wizard's staff seen in movies. It fired a single blast that emitted a massive ball of fire. The fire hurled itself at the group, but Lucas stretched his hands forward and created a wall of ice to block the attack.

"Interesting," the hostile said to Lucas. It seemed a bit surprised, yet pleased at the same time.

"Yeah, well guess what, he isn't the only one!" Mia stretched her hands forward and concentrated heavily. Suddenly the door of the classroom next to the hostile ripped off the hinges and hit the hostile square in the head. The hostile dropped the staff weapon and hit the ground with a loud thud.

Mia quickly stretched her hands forward and used her telekinesis to bring the staff weapon to her. The hostile reached for it, but the weapon moved towards Mia with great velocity.

James quickly grabbed a ladder in the hallway and ran forward. He swung it with ease like a baseball bat and connected with great force. The hostile flew backwards and went through a classroom.

Lucas and Mia moved with urgency and caught up with James. The three of them cautiously approached the room the hostile fell into.

"Careful," Mia said as Lucas took the lead.

"Move," James suddenly shouted. James pushed Lucas out of the way just in the nick of time. He quickly shifted his feet forward and with his right arm, shattered a desk the hostile heaved in their direction.

The hostile studied the three Post Humans and smiled. "Cyrokinesis, Telekinesis and Superhuman strength. So the stories are true. You are indeed the next generation."

Lucas, James and Mia did not understand what the hostile was talking about and at that moment, none of them cared. The only thing on their mind was stopping the intruder from causing any more harm. It was a task that proved to be quite daunting.

"Who are you, what do you want?" Mia shouted.

"Those questions will be answered in due time."

"What's the play?" Mia whispered to James.

James stared the hostile down. The hostile seemed completely unfazed by their presence.

"Hit him with everything we've got."

"Him?" Lucas echoed.

James thought for a moment and shrugged his shoulders. "Okay, let's be real, what we're looking at isn't human. What we're looking at isn't even a Post Human, that right there is an alien. A male alien, so yeah, hit him with everything we got!"

"All right, let's do this!" Mia said.

James charged forward while Mia and Lucas stretched their hands and unleashed their respective powers on the red skinned alien.

The alien easily caught James by the throat, lifted him off the ground, and threw him into the nearest wall. The alien showed a complete disregard for James' presence. As Lucas' ice attack and the force of Mia's telekinesis approached, the alien calmly reached to his left wrist and activated a personal force field.

"Your abilities have no effects on me," the alien said. Mia and Lucas stopped their attack and rethought their plan. Satisfied by their reaction, the alien snickered and deactivated his force field.

"You sure we have no effect on you?" James asked. The alien turned just in time to see James' fist connect with a devastating uppercut that sent the alien flying backwards. James rushed over to the alien and delivered several closed fists punches to various parts of the alien's body. With punches as hard as a rock, James disabled the personal force field.

The alien embraced James' attack and waited for the slightest opening. When he found one, the alien pushed James off of him and reached for his staff weapon. "Lucas, freeze him!" James said.

Lucas stretched his hands forward and directed a massive ice attack large enough to completely encase the alien.

"Should we finish him off?" Mia asked.

"Yeah," James replied.

The encased alien concentrated and slowly the ice began to crack. Before the trio could reach him, the alien broke free. He looked around the room and saw the three Post Humans ready to make another move on him, but with his force field disabled, he did not want to take any chances.

"This isn't over!" The alien drove his hands downward and hit the ground with such force that the entire area around him collapsed to the first floor. The alien emerged from the debris and fled the school, leaving behind his staff weapon. Mia, James and Lucas watched the alien leave the school through one of the back doors.

"Should we go after him?" Mia asked.

James listened to the sounds of several police cars approaching. "No time, with our luck, they could be after us."

"Lucas, where are you going?" Mia shouted.

Lucas used his cyrokinesis ability and created an ice slide which he used to easily descend to the first floor. "Away from you two. You guys do nothing but bring trouble. I know it's not intentional, but everywhere you go, trouble follows!"

Lucas did not look back. He ran out of the school as fast as he could. He had no intentions on going after the alien, but he had no intentions on sticking around for questions either.

"Lucas wait!" Mia was about to chase after Lucas on the ice slide, but before she could slide down, James lifted her by the waist and stopped her. "What are you doing James? We have to go after him!"

"There's no time Mia, Lucas made his decision."

"He's just scared!"

"That may be true, but we have to leave. We can track him down later, but we have to get out of here." James and Mia could hear the footsteps of officers coming up the stairs. Begrudgingly, Mia had no choice but to let Lucas go his separate way. "Tommy, get the ship ready!" James said into his earpiece.

"Already on it, you guys going to make it?"

"Yeah we got it, be there in a minute." James looked around the room for a way out. He could hear the police closing in on their position and feared there was no way to avoid a confrontation.

James sighed. He could hear police officers down on the first floor inspecting the ice slide while several more cautiously made their way up the stairs. "Come on Mia, grab the staff weapon and let's go."

Mia angrily grabbed the staff weapon and walked over to James. She jumped into his arms and rolled her eyes. "I feel like such a cliché every time we do this."

"You're more than welcome to do this on your own. Although I don't think your particular skill set will work as effectively."

"Just shut up and get us out of here, will ya?"

"Stop right there and place your hands in the air!" the first officer to reach the room shouted. James and Mia turned towards the door where the officer stood with his weapon pointed.

"Mia," James said.

"On it." Mia flicked her wrist and with the force of her telekinesis, knocked the officer's weapon out of his hand.

With Mia still in his arms, James jumped through the window and shattered it into several pieces. The first two officers to make it to the room ran towards the window to see the results of James' jump.

"No way, that's impossible!" one officer said.

He looked down and saw that James and Mia landed safely without so much of a scratch on them. "The impact of that jump alone should've broken his legs!" The officers watched in complete shock as the Ascendants' cloaked ship slowly shimmered into visibility.

"Let's go Christine, get us out of here!" James shouted.

Christine needed no prompt from James or anyone else for that matter. As soon as James and Mia boarded the ship, Christine placed her hands back on the throttle and navigated through the skies.

"Lou, did you see that? What the heck did I just see?" one officer asked.

Lou swallowed spit and watched the plane vanish out of sight. "Our worst fears... Post Humans with enough power to destroy us all."

Chapter 7

Presidential Address

"Yes sir, I understand," Christine said. Christine ended the phone call and slid her phone back into her pocket.

"What is it?" James asked.

Christine did her best to hide her concern, but James could see right through her.

"Christine?" James said.

"Dr. Connors said there was trouble. He didn't elaborate but from his tone, I can tell it's bad, it's really bad."

James and Mia looked at one another with troubled expressions.

"I shouldn't have left them alone. A mission as risky as that, I should have gone with them."

"Well, at the risk of sounding selfish, I'm glad you didn't. I don't think Lucas and I would have made it out of the school if you weren't there with us."

"I'm sure you two would've gotten out all right."

"You could just be thinking the worst James,

after what we encountered today, it's not so hard to imagine that you might be on edge. We don't even know what happened yet."

"Christine and James are right, something terrible did happen," Tori said suddenly.

Christine, Tommy, James and Mia whipped their heads around to face Tori, who emerged from her private quarters.

"Tori, what's wrong?" Tommy asked.
Tori's face was pale and she could barely stand up straight.

"Tori?" James said.

James rushed over towards Tori and grabbed her before she collapsed to the ground. Tommy ran over on the other side and helped James get her back to her feet. Even though James was more than capable of lifting Tori himself, Tommy still felt it was the right thing to do.

"She's dead," Tori moaned.

James and Tommy walked Tori over a seat in the control room while Mia fetched her a bottle of water.

"Who's dead?" James asked.

"Susan."

The room fell deadly silent. Everyone looked around at one another but no one knew what to say.

"Tori, what are you talking about? What happened to Susan?" Mia asked.

Drained from the strenuous telepathy she had used, Tori moaned and grabbed her head.

"Tori, what happened?" James asked. He snapped his fingers to get her attention.

"I don't know; I just know I can no longer read Susan's mind. I've searched and searched but I can't read it."

"What about Dr. Connors, what about Cayde?" James asked.

"Both of them are overcome with grief. Both of them are trying to process what happened. They're in shock."

James and Mia looked towards one another. They both read each other's mind without the use of telepathy.

"Don't do it," Tori said.

"We have to Tori. Christine, pick up the pace!" James and Mia left the control room and retreated to the armory. Unsure what they would deal with, the two Post Humans equipped themselves with enough armor and ammunition to fight a small war.

Christine was landing the ship when James and Mia reappeared from the armory.

"Don't you think you two should wait for backup?" Tommy asked.

"Tommy, we are backup," James replied. The ship landed safely and smoothly. James took the lead and without hesitation left the ship with his gun drawn. Mia followed closely behind him and watched his six.

"See anything?" Mia asked.

"Nothing."

Mia pulled out her phone and checked the GPS tracker. "Dr. Connors signal tracks him here to this location."

"Doesn't mean he's in there and it doesn't mean we aren't walking into a trap. Stay on your toes Mia."

James raised his gun and cautiously moved towards a house in the final stages of construction. "Dr. Connors?" James called out.

"We're up here!" Dr. Connors replied.

James and Mia looked at one another and for a moment were filled with relief. Ever the cautious one, James kept his gun in hand and slowly walked up the stairs. Mia followed closely behind and kept her eyes in the other direction just in case they were still walking into an ambush.

"Up here, hurry!" Dr. Connors said. James whipped inside the room where Dr. Connors voice came from and quickly checked it out. "We're alone son, you can put the gun away."

James did one more survey of his surroundings before cautiously sliding his gun back in its holster. He looked over towards Cayde and his face suddenly went flush. "No, no, no!" James cried.

Cayde sat somberly in the left corner of the

room with Susan's lifeless body cradled across his lap.

James ran over to him and dropped to his knees. He stroked Susan's medium length black hair, and a tear fell from his eye. James turned and looked directly down on Dr. Connors. "What happened?"

"I'll explain back on the ship, but we need to get out of here right now."

James placed his arm behind the back of Susan's head and lifted her off Cayde's lap. Tears flowed from Mia's face as she watched James pass her by. She bit her lip and did her best not to let her emotions completely run away from her.

"Guys, radio chatter is running rampant. Squad cars will be at our position within minutes. We need to go," Tommy said over the group's connected earpieces.

"We're on our way out now, be ready to move as soon as we board," Dr. Connors said.

James carried Susan all the way down the stairs and out of the house. The hangar bay door opened, and the group followed James back to the ship. Tommy immediately dropped to the ground and cried as soon as he saw Susan. James choked up. He fought back the tears that swelled in the corner of his eyes and walked right passed the group.

"Where is he going?" Tommy asked.

"He's taking her back to her room," Mia replied. She knew James well enough to predict exactly what he was going to do and why he would do it in that particular way.

Christine pulled on the throttle and ascended to the skies as James left the room.

"What happened?" Mia asked.

"Commander Sullivan is what happened. I knew those guys couldn't be trusted," Cayde said.

"Now wait a minute Cayde, we don't know that for sure. We don't know what happened exactly," Dr. Connors said.

James returned from Susan's room after gently placing her in her bed. "What do you mean you don't know?" he asked in a voice slightly deeper than his usual tone.

Dr. Connors was startled by James. He knew James was extremely protective and looked after the group with everything he had in him. He knew James was feeling a lot of guilt in that moment for not being there by Susan's side.

"Who killed her and how did she die?" James asked.

"We don't know who killed her but we do know how. She was killed by a sniper," Dr. Connors said.

Cayde gritted his teeth. "A sniper on Commander Sullivan's payroll!"

"I knew going there was a bad idea!" James said. James slammed his fist into one of the tables in the control center and completely shattered it.

"James, take it down a notch. I cannot say with

certainty that Commander Sullivan had anything to do with what happened to Susan. I refuse to believe a government representing the United States would so callously kill an American citizen without just cause."

"Who's to say they truly represent the United States? Perhaps this is some shadow group working within the government but not necessarily authorized by the government," Christine said.

Dr. Connors sighed. "Such groups exist?"

"You better believe it. There are so many agencies within our country alone that technically don't exist. Groups authorized by certain factions within the government, but do everything off books, that way the government can keep their hands clean. This very easily could've been a group acting on orders secretly."

"Wait, you guys, quiet down!" Mia said.

"Mia, what is it?" James asked.

Mia pointed to the television and stared at it.

"Tommy, turn it up," James said.
Tommy positioned his hands on the keyboard, and turned the volume up.

"Good evening my fellow Americans."

The Ascendants' eyes and ears were glued to the television. They waited nervously to hear what the President had to say.

"Today is a day that many of us feared for a while now. As you know, it's been a little over a year since the existence of Post Humans became public. Immediately the world became fascinated and terrified with this revelation. For decades the world has wondered is there life beyond the stars. Never had we imagined that the truly extraordinary existence that would change our way of life was right here on our own planet. Since that fateful day, many have wondered and worried about the state of our nation and the security risks in which these Post Humans pose. With each day that passes, more and more individuals seem to pop up with the extra gene in them."

Dr. Connors and Christine shared an unspoken but definitely recognizable worried look.

"My administration has been very proactive in monitoring Post Human activity and as such we've learned various ways to handle Post Humans that break the law. And believe me when I say, Post Humans will be held at the same degree as those without abilities. If a Post Human breaks the law, they will pay the price just like any one of us."

James cracked his knuckles and looked as if he was ready for a fight.

"They're going to declare war on us," Cayde said to James.

"Let them try!"

"Quiet down you two," Dr. Connors said.
An image of the scene that took place early that morning involving Cooper Barrett and the

government agents flashed on the screen. The image prompted the President to speak on the matter.

"Within the past few months, we've seen an uptick of criminal activity within the Post Human community. Just this morning, a Post Human terrorist by the name of Cooper Barrett sought out to cause serious harm to the citizens of this great nation. His attack this morning killed one and injured twelve. His attack pushed the fears many of us have regarding the Post Humans' presence. I am here to address those fears."

The President looked over to his left and nodded. A large man with slick gray hair and biceps the size of tree trunks walked up to the podium and joined the President.

"Well the plot certainly thickens. That's Commander Sullivan," Cayde said.

"Due to the risk Post Humans pose and the alarming number of cases involving Post Humans abusing their abilities, I have authorized the creation of a very specific organization."

The President looked over to Commander Sullivan and nodded. The Commander nodded back. "To my left is Commander Sullivan. A highly decorated veteran who has given well over thirty years of his life serving this great nation. I have given this man the incredibly challenging task of policing Post Human activity. Government, Units,

Against, Radical, Danger, or simply G.U.A.R.D. will keep these criminals in line. Rest assured that if a problem occurs within your community and a Post Human is behind the disturbance, Commander Sullivan and his agents will be there to stop them."

"G.U.A.R.D., what kind of name is that?" Cayde asked.

"The kind of name someone uses when they really want their acronym to be catchy," Tommy replied.

Cayde chuckled slightly and turned his attention back to the screen.

"In addition to the situation involving Cooper Barrett, it has been reported that another Post Human attacked a school killing three individuals."

"That's not true, it wasn't a Post Human," Mia said.

Dr. Connors looked at Mia concernedly. "What school, what is he talking about?"

Mia shook her head. "We'll have to fill you in on that later." She looked over to James, who looked over to Dr. Connors and nodded.

Dr. Connors sighed heavily. His heart and mind were already feeling the weight of the world; he didn't know how much more he could take.

"Some of these Post Humans have taken our kindness for weakness. Some of these Post Humans believe their abilities make them better than the rest of us. I am here to remind them that we are the people of the United States of America. We the people can overcome any obstacles and challenges thrown our way. We will not be intimidated and we will not be submissive. If you abuse your abilities, we are coming for you. We are one nation and we are one people, and we will not be afraid!"

The President paused to let the thunderous applauds take place. For two minutes he stood there and smiled. "Thank you all and God bless America."

The President did not bother to take any questions from the media. As soon as he concluded his speech, he turned around and walked back through the double doors, leaving the entire world to digest his powerful words.

Dr. Connors adjusted his glasses and frowned. "Turn it off."

Tommy pressed the corresponding button on his keyboard and the big screen in the center of the control room went blank.

Cayde looked around the room anxiously. He hated awkward moments and an entire room of people saying absolutely nothing was about as awkward as it got for him. "Well this certainly wasn't the way I pictured the day going when I woke up this morning." Cayde hoped for a response from the group, but they were too filled with concern to react to Cayde's obvious need to eradicate the awkwardness in the room.

Dr. Connors ignored Cayde and looked directly over towards Mia. His face was scrunched and his throat felt awfully dry. "What were you talking about just a minute ago? What do you know about the attack at the school?"

Mia had an apprehensive look on her face. As always when she felt unsure, she turned to James for decisiveness.

"The attack that took place at the school is the same place we just came from," James said.

Dr. Connors raised his eyebrow. "Did you two have something to do with that?" He hated the fact that he even had to ask that question, but he knew anything could've gone wrong and the situation could've easily changed from casual to deadly.

"No, no, we had absolutely nothing to do with that attack!" Mia said shaking her head repeatedly. "Well I mean, we did have something to do with it, but not in the way that you think. Like, we didn't start the attack on any civilians or anything like that, but we were definitely involved."

Dr. Connors stared at Mia with his mouth open in disbelief. "I have no idea what the heck you're talking about. What happened at the school?"

"We ran into some trouble. We found Lucas, and he had no interest at all in coming back with us or helping us in any way. Before I had the chance to use a more persuasive approach, we heard screaming. So I went to check it out and I couldn't believe what I saw."

Cayde's ears perked up. "What did you see?"

"A monster," Mia said.

James gave Mia a less than amused look. "An alien, we saw a seven foot, red skinned, long dreadlock wearing, massively built alien. The alien used some sort of staff weapon the likes of which I've never seen. He took on our combined abilities without breaking a sweat."

The room filled with another awkward silence. Dr. Connors wet his lips and did his best to remain calm. "I honestly don't know what's worst. The situation with this G.U.A.R.D. agency or your so called alien."

"You think they're covering the existence of this alien up?" Cayde asked.

"I don't think so," Dr. Connors said.

"Actually, I'm pretty sure they are covering it up. I noticed the change in demeanor when he mentioned Post Human in conjunction with the school. He knew he was telling a lie, and it bothered him," Christine said.

"Yeah, well it bothered me too. That staff weapon literally burned a hole right through the body of some unsuspecting teacher."

"We are way in over our heads!" Cayde said. Cayde looked around the room. He looked at the bruises James and Mia acquired battling the alien,

Tori's massive headache from using her telepathy and locating abilities too much. He noticed the weary expression on Dr. Connors face and the shaky hands Christine was trying to hide. The Ascendants were in complete disarray and it worried him.

"You're right Cayde, we are way in over our heads." Dr. Connors reached in the breast pocket of his suit, pulled out a handkerchief and wiped his glasses. He looked around the room. His eyes connected with each member of the group and smiled. "When I first started this group, I had no idea what I was doing. I had no idea how I was going to find you or even more so, how I was going to protect you."

Dr. Connors locked in on Tori. "Then I found Tori. Be it luck or sheer destiny, Tori's abilities allowed me to track down others. I was able to find people who based on her review were like-minded individuals. With every single one of you, my confidence grew, and I knew we had the makings of something really special. We stayed underground, we remained quiet, and we trained. Now granted, I've seen some pretty powerful Post Humans out there, but I've never seen a group as committed to one another as you guys are."

Cayde rubbed his face. He knew Dr. Connors' words were supposed to be motivational, but after the day they had, he wasn't feeling too motivated.

About the only motivation he had at that moment was to leave.

"What exactly are we supposed to do Dr. Connors? I mean your speech is all fine and dandy, but the fact remains we have a huge target on our back. How are we supposed to take on highly trained government agents and superior aliens?"

"We do it together," a familiar voice said. The group nearly broke their necks as they turned their heads towards the control room's entrance. They stared in disbelief and stood still.

Finally, James made a move forward. He studied the individual carefully. James raised his right hand forward and reached for the individual's face, but the intended target quickly grabbed James' wrist and twisted it downward.

"If you value that arm, then I suggest you keep your hands to yourself," the individual said. The two shared an intense stare. Neither of them blinked or batted an eye.

"Is it you? Is it really you?" Tommy asked.

"Of course it's me, who else were you expecting?"

"Pretty much anyone but you," Cayde said.

The individual looked at Cayde with a completely perplexed expression. "Why?"

Dr. Connors stepped forward. His face as white as a ghost and his mouth as dry as the desert. "Because Susan, you're supposed to be dead."

Epilogue

After his battle with James, Mia, and Lucas, the red skinned alien safely retreated to his ship and returned to the dark side of the moon. He had a plethora of advanced technology at his disposal, including technology that concealed his presence from Earth's satellites and long range sensors.

While the alien's home world was several million light years away, the moon served as his staging area. For months the alien occupied the moon, monitoring human activity and recording all of it to his superior.

The alien grimaced slightly as he walked to his private quarters and took off his armor. He laid his stuff neatly on the nightstand next to his bed and strolled over to a small table on the opposite side of his bed. He reached inside the small compartment located on the right side of the table and took out two small devices.

The first device was in the shape of a square. It was see-through and on the inside were a number of intricate electronic parts that would've been difficult for the majority of the people of earth and the alien's home world to comprehend.

The alien pressed the small triangular button on the left side of the device and held it to his body. He relaxed as the device activated and quickly went to work repairing any bodily damage he suffered during his altercation with the Post Humans.

It took all of two minutes for the device to heal his wounds. Once the device finished doing its job, the alien returned the device to its spot in his drawer and picked up the other device.

The second device was slightly larger in size and shaped triangularly with jagged edges. Unlike the first device, this one wasn't see-through, but its insides were just as intricate as the first. The alien activated the device and waited patiently for a response.

Seconds later, a live holographic image of another red skinned alien emerged. "Supreme Commander, I bring news on the humans," the alien said. He stood tall, nodded, and bowed before his leader.

"Rise Azir," the Supreme Commander said. Azir rose to his feet and waited patiently to be granted permission to speak.

While Azir was quite intimidating in stature and looks to the Ascendants, he was nothing more than a scientist on his home world. Azir stood near seven feet tall while his superior was nearly a foot taller and even larger.

"What news of the human world do you bring?"

"My lord, I have just recently returned from battle. I encountered three humans with abilities."

The Supreme Commander smiled. Sharp jagged, brown stained teeth flashed. In the background what looked like hundreds more of Azir's kind stopped what they were doing and listened in on the conversation. "Go on."

"My lord, I battled two of the male species and one female. They each possessed a different ability."

"What sort of abilities did these humans possess?"

Azir thought back to his battle. "One male, dark skin and built rather strong for a human possessed increased strength."

The Supreme Commander snickered. He felt there was no equal in regards to strength when it came to his oppositions. "How strong could he have possibly been?"

"Nowhere near as strong as you my lord and nowhere near as strong as the Genoshians."

The word "Genoshians," always evoked a strong reaction from the Supreme Commander. In fact, it evoked a strong reaction out of just about every Ashtarian that ever lived.

Azir continued. "I do need to say that while this particular human displayed a power set far less superior to ours, I have seen on the thing they call a television, others that certainly can rival our strength my lord."

The Supreme Commander did not like the sound of that. He gritted his teeth and began to pace around the command center of his massive warship. "What of the other two you encountered?"

"The other male, he seemed to know the two he battled with, but from what I could tell, he was not with them. I do not know how to explain it, but I know that when the battle was over, he left alone."

"What can he do?"

Azir thought back to his encounter. Out of the three it was Lucas that impressed him the most. "He was able to manipulate ice. He produced ice from his body and used it to trap me."

The Supreme Commander cocked his head slightly. He turned around and spoke in another language to the navigational officer before turning back to face Azir. "You were encased in ice?"

"Yes, my lord."

"This human produced ice from within himself. There was no sort of technology used to aid him?"

Azir nodded. "As far as I could tell my lord, the human possessed no such device to mimic such abilities. He did it himself."

"And what about the female?"

Azir thought of Mia and smiled. "The female, while little in stature, she possessed a big heart. She reminds me of our female warriors. This woman was able to move objects just by thinking about them. She would flick her wrist and objects around her would move however she decided to manipulate them. I believe they call it telekinesis."

The Supreme Commander growled loudly and began barking out orders to everyone aboard the ship. "Is there anything else?"

"The humans without these abilities grow leery of those with them. As a result, the government of this world has formed an agency designed to battle these humans with abilities and put them away if need be. In my opinion, matters between these two groups of humans will continue to deteriorate to the point that a civil war of sorts will occur."

The Supreme Commander nodded his head forward and smiled. He thought to himself for a moment and while he thought, no one on his ship moved a muscle. "So it's true, the descendants of the Genoshians really do reside on Earth. The second generation walks amongst the stars and they have no clue the lineage in which they come from."

Azir pulled up an image on his computer. Using sophisticated, stolen technology from an extremely intellectual race of beings, Azir was able to monitor all of Earth's satellites and communications without being detected.

"What is it Azir, what do you see?" the Supreme Commander asked.

"Opportunity."

The Supreme Commander let out a loud and sadistic laugh. "Indeed Azir, opportunity indeed!"

"My lord, how shall I proceed?"

The Supreme Commander sat back in his chair and thought for a moment. His thoughts were interrupted when the weapons officer notified him of an incoming attack. Three long range missiles shot forward and attacked the Supreme Commander's vessel. "Shields up." The ship rocked slightly from the impact of the missiles. "Status report?"

"Shields holding at ninety-nine percent my lord," one of the monitors stated.

The Supreme Commander smiled. "Good." He moved forward and looked out the window at two hostile ships. One on the left and the other on the right. "Show these pathetic beings the might of the Ashtarian empire."

The monitor smiled. "With pleasure my lord." The monitor looked towards the weapon's operator and nodded. The weapon's operator nodded back and armed the ships primary weapons. With a click of a button, a red plasma like energy torpedoed out of the warship and headed straight for the two enemy vessels.

The red plasma hit the two ships and ripped through its defenses with minimal effort. The red plasma engulfed both ships and within minutes, the two vessels exploded into millions of pieces.

Satisfied with the outcome, the Supreme Commander turned back to face Azir. "The humans might have abilities now, but they have no idea what they're up against. Continue to monitor the human's progress and be ready for my signal. Soon we will destroy the Earth and repopulate it with our people."

"Yes my lord, as you command it."

The Supreme Commander stared out into the stars. His mind filled with thoughts of galactic glory. "Soon the Earth will be ours!"

Sneak Peek

Below is a sneak peek at one of the many adventures of two superheroes from the League of Protectors, Jackson Prescott and Shayne Tucker. Enjoy!

The League of Protectors: Fire and Ice

"Okay guys, this interview is going to be pretty laid back. I've compiled a list of my personal questions for you, along with questions submitted by our viewers," Alicia Torres said to Shayne and Jackson.

Alicia Torres was a year older than Shayne and Jackson. She was an aspiring journalist who was a lead reporter for Jackson and Shayne's school's weekly paper. For over a year, she had been trying to schedule an interview with the duo and for over a year, the crime-fighting duo had to reschedule.

Her time had finally come though. It was the day in which she would finally be able to interview the duo and really try to learn more about them. She was excited and nervous all at the same time. She wasn't the only one though, Shayne was unusually nervous as well.

He wasn't the biggest fan of giving interviews, but it wasn't as if he was nervous or shy when he did give them. This particular day though, something was different. Jackson noted it took Shayne much longer than normal to get ready. Typically, it was Jackson that spent nearly an hour in the shower each day. But on this occasion it was Shayne that was hogging the bathroom.

"Do you guys have any questions before we get started?" Alicia asked.

Jackson looked towards Shayne and let out a slight chuckle. He could see that Shayne was trying to hide his attraction for Alicia.

Shayne was dressed up even more than usual. It wasn't as if this was the first interview they had given, or an interview with special significance, neither was the case. This was simply a school interview. Jackson now understood why Shayne was overdressed.

Jackson looked down at himself and noticed a stark difference in the way in which he was dressed compared to Shayne. Jackson was in a blue tank top and some old blue jean shorts. Shayne on the other hand was dressed in a long sleeve button down shirt, black vest, and well pressed dark blue jeans.

"Interesting," Jackson said.

"I'm sorry?" Alicia said turning her attention towards Jackson.

"I do have a question before we get started," Jackson said his eyes switched between Alicia and Shayne.

Jackson and Shayne's bond was so close; people often thought the two shared a telepathic link, as both men were often able to decipher each other's thoughts, just by looking at one another. Shayne already knew what Jackson was up to and it made him slightly nervous.

"OK, go ahead," Alicia said.

"I was just curious, which lucky guy around here has the privilege of calling you his girl?" Jackson asked.

Alicia was surprised by the question. Her slightly pale face turned three shades of red. "I'm currently focusing on my classes right now. Looking towards my career," she finally said without looking either man in the eye.

Jackson chuckled. "So basically... you're single?" Alicia laughed uncomfortably and acknowledged that Jackson was correct. "You hear that bro? She's single," Jackson said he looked at Shayne. It was now Shayne's turn to turn three shades redder.

"Let's get started with the interview," Shayne replied. He desperately wanted the conversation to change immediately.

"I agree," Alicia said, smiling politely. She let her gaze linger on Shayne just a second longer than it should have. Alicia looked towards her cameraman for confirmation that he was ready to proceed. The cameraman gave a slight nod, prompting Alicia to begin the interview.

"Good morning, I'm here with Jackson Prescott and Shayne Tucker, two of the most prominent Post Humans in the world today. Gentlemen, it's an absolute pleasure to have this opportunity to interview you."

"It's great to be here. We love this country. We love our fans and we love doing what we do," Jackson said flashing his million-dollar smile.

"I've had a chance to check out your articles, you do excellent work. I have no doubt in my mind that you're going to make an excellent journalist someday," Shayne added with his typical chill demeanor and tone.

Alicia smiled brightly. She appreciated the compliment tremendously. She thanked Shayne for the kind words and then proceeded on with the interview.

"First question, what is a typical day like for the League of Protectors?"

Jackson looked over towards Shayne. Typically, it was Shayne that answered the first question in any of the duos' interviews. That pattern held true on this day as well.

"Well first off, I think it's important that everyone that watches this interview realizes that we are humans just like the rest of the world. We just happen to have extraordinary abilities and as such, we've been given a different classification. Sometimes I really hate the word Post Humans because it's a label, and labels can be destructive and divisive at times. It's like when people look at me and they classify me as a young black man. I hate that, I'm a man, my skin tone is just a part of who I am, but it doesn't define me," Shayne said.

Alicia smiled as Shayne spoke. She found him to be very eloquent in his speech. She had heard several of his interviews before, but it was truly impressive to listen to him speak in person.

"With that said, each of us lives our lives as best as we can. This is our second year in college now. My concentration is on genetics. I'm really curious to learn more about how these extra genes humans possess are activate in some, but not in others. The phenomenon that is Post Humans has really expanded the field of genetic research. It's mind boggling how little we really know about the field."

"I'm currently undecided in my career choice. Although a career in Hollywood doesn't sound too bad," Jackson chimed in.

Alicia smiled politely. "I can see you playing yourself in some Hollywood movie."
Jackson laughed loudly; he could easily see himself playing the role of himself in a movie.

"All of us have responsibilities beyond protecting this country. Making sure beautiful women like you stay safe, is a top priority of ours," Jackson said.

"Making sure everyone stays safe is a top priority of ours," Shayne clarified, he wanted to make sure he corrected what would obviously be viewed as a sexist statement by Jackson.

"Yeah, that's what I said," Jackson retorted.

"Okay, moving on, next question comes from one of our fellow students here on campus. Jim, a junior, wants to know how do you balance your time being a member of the League and also a college sophomore?"

Shayne thought for a moment. Jim's question was a good one as balancing the two "jobs" wasn't easy.

"It's about prioritizing. There's no telling when our name is going to be called, there's no telling when our presence is going to be needed. Me personally, I try to stay ahead of my schoolwork so that when I'm needed, I don't find myself falling behind. It's not easy balancing the two, but I make as conscious an effort as possible to do so."

"Yeah, I just try to live in the moment. Life is too short. Every time I do battle with someone, there's a chance it could be my last. So I just try to live everyday carefree and enjoy it while I can. I know some people think that's a bad idea. That by doing so, I'm not being productive enough with my education. But I am who I am, and I refuse to let society dictate my happiness," Jackson said.

"Great answers. Next question, how long have you two been friends and what makes your bond so tight?"

The duo looked towards one another and smiled with respect. "We've been friends since we were little," Jackson started. "We went to the same private school together. We lived nearby. We played the same sports. We just, we were just meant to be the best of friends. I mean our friendship is the stuff of legend. It's legendare..."

"Don't do it!" Shayne chimed in.

"It's legendary!" Jackson finished, paying homage to his favorite show, "How I Met Your Mother."

"I loved that show! I was sad when it went off the air," Alicia said with a jubilant facial expression.

Shayne at that moment felt a bit out of the loop as he had never seen the appeal of that show. Then again, he had never watched an episode in its entirety. Perhaps he would have to go back, watch it, and give it another chance.

"But in all seriousness, while Shayne and I might be opposites in a lot of ways, there's nobody that gets me better than Shayne does. This guy right here is my brother. My brother from another mother."

Shayne rolled his eyes. He hated that expression and found it corny, like he did most of Jackson's expressions.

"It shows that you two are close. The way you guys work together on the field is intriguing to watch. You two really complement each other well and it's so cool that even your abilities are polar opposites!"

"Okay, I've been saving this question here for the ladies. All of our female viewers are dying to know if you are seeing anyone, and if not, what qualities do you look for in a woman?"

Jackson looked towards Shayne to see if he wanted to answer the question first, as he expected, Shayne did not.

"I'll be real with you Ms. Torres, what I look for in a woman is someone that's smoking hot! Black, White, Hispanic, Asian, race doesn't mean anything to me. What matters is that she's hot," Jackson said. "And having some sort of personality is beneficial as well," he added.

The look on Alicia's face indicated she was surprised by Jackson's honesty. Jackson shrugged his shoulders and smiled with that charmed grin of his. "Hey, I like to keep it one hundred."

"I've never really understood that phrase," Alicia replied. She felt a little embarrassed that she didn't understand that popular phrase that was seen on social media sites all the time.

"It simply means he likes to tell the truth. He likes to be honest about what he's thinking. One hundred percent," Shayne said.

"My answer reflects what a lot of guys feel, but don't want to say. They don't want to come across as shallow. Screw it. Call me shallow. I don't care, I'm just being real. I hope whatever woman I hook up with has a great personality. But the first thing I look at is how attractive she is."

Alicia looked towards her cameraman who was still trying to regain his composure thanks to Jackson's comments. "How about you Mr. Tucker, do you share a similar opinion as Mr. Prescott?"

There was something about the way in which Alicia asked the question that peeked Jackson's interest. It was almost as if she was asking for Shayne's perspective on a personal level and not necessarily as a journalist.

"Like most things about us, Shayne is the complete opposite on this subject as well. He's one of those hopeless romantics!" Jackson said. He leaned in and placed his arm playfully around Shayne's shoulder.

Alicia smiled, she liked what she heard, but she still wanted to hear it from Shayne himself.

"If anyone ever told you that looks don't matter, they aren't being completely honest with you. An individual has to have some level of attraction to another for a relationship to work. However, for me, a woman's personality means everything. Her values, her beliefs, her opinions, everything that makes her who she is on the inside is what I look for. It's what's needed to keep my interest. A woman's physical beauty is an added bonus, but my perfect woman starts from the inside and then out," Shayne said.

Jackson rolled his eyes and chuckled. "Ladies,

this guy right here is as genuine as it gets. I kid you not, everything he just said, he truly means!"

Not only was Jackson quite skilled in combat and picking up women, he was also one fantastic wing man. If Shayne allowed him to do so more often, the number of women Jackson could've landed for him would've been much higher.

The cameraman snapped his fingers lightly to gain Alicia's attention. He gestured for her to wrap the interview up.

"OK guys, we have time for one final question, the thing everyone wants to know is..."

A symphony of panicked screams interrupted Alicia. Outside of the gym where the interview was taking place, several frantic students scurried about trying to avoid the wrath of two intruders.

"Did we miss the interview?" one of the intruders asked. The speaker was short; he stood at about five feet seven inches. His hair was long, shaggy and black, his skin peach.

"Nope, looks like you arrived just in time!" Jackson said, hopping out of his seat and taking a defensive stance. "You're going to want to get this," Jackson said to the cameraman before he turned his attention back to the two intruders. The two intruders headed towards the duo.

"You two looking for your fifteen minutes of fame?" Jackson asked. "Well probably more like five, because that's about as long as I suspect it'll take to handle the likes of you."

Shayne raised his eyebrow at that last statement. While the first speaker did not have an imposing look, the other individual did.

Standing at five feet, ten inches, the man was built like a bull. Shayne took a defensive stance and waited patiently for the two men to make a move. For the time being, the League members were at a disadvantage. Everyone that was interested in combating members of the League knew their skill set, but Shayne and Jackson had no idea what these two individuals were capable of.

The duo had three options. They could call Stephanie and get an idea of who they were dealing with, they could run a facial recognition program, or they could find out the old fashioned way. While the first two options were more ideal, there wasn't enough time to go through the process required to get that information.

"Before we take you out, mind telling us your names?" Jackson asked confidently.

The big bull looking man wasn't in the mood to talk. He was there to fight, and fight is what he did.

The man lowered his head and charged forward.

"Would you look at that? Not only is this guy built like a bull, but he comes charging at me like one as well!" Jackson said looking into the camera.

Jackson waited until the charging man was close

enough to him that he wouldn't be able to slow down his momentum. When the man got close enough, Jackson created a wall of ice that the bullish looking man foolishly ran straight into. "You would think he would've seen that one coming!" Jackson said into the camera.

"Focus!" Shayne snapped.

"I'm focusing on how incredibly stupid these two are!" Jackson replied back. "So, how does it feel to get an exclusive video of a Jackson Prescott and Shayne Tucker epic battle?" Jackson asked Alicia.

"Jackson, look out!" Shayne hollered. Shayne sped over towards Jackson and pushed him out of the way just as a bolt of electricity was about to strike him. Shayne grimaced as he caught a fraction of the lightning bolt.

"Crap, you okay bro?" Jackson asked.

"Yeah, nothing my healing factor won't fix, neutralize him before he gets off another electric shot," Shayne ordered. He took charge as he always did.

"So, electric shock is his ability," Jackson said to himself as he charged forward towards the young man trying to electrocute him. Shayne and Jackson still had no idea what the man that was built like a bull could do besides run foolishly into ice walls, but unfortunately, they would soon find out.

While Shayne made his way back to his feet, the

bullish looking man had already recovered. He stealthily snuck up from behind Shayne and wrapped him in a bear hug. Shayne could feel his bones crushing. He desperately fought back to get the man off of him. Having no other option and on the verge of succumbing to the pain, Shayne heated himself up making it impossible for the bullish man to hold on to him.

"Whoops miss me!" Jackson said showing a lack of respect for his opponent. Jackson constructed an ice sled and moved around on it swerving left and right to evade the dark-haired man's attack.

"Jackson!" Shayne shouted angrily as bolts of electricity zipped passed him, Alicia, the cameraman and the bullish looking man.

"On it!" Jackson shouted back as he hopped off the ice constructed sled. He hopped off in such a way that the sled came spiraling towards the dark haired man. The dark haired man was able to evade the creative attack, but Jackson followed right back and made the ground beneath the man's feet slippery.

"Caution, wet floor!" Jackson mocked as the man tumbled to the ground. Jackson took his time approaching the dark haired man. With one last attempt, the man stretched his hands forward and released a weak blast of electricity, the man's aim was off and the shot missed.

"Oh, so close!" Jackson said with fake sympathy.

He reached down inside his pocket and pulled out the inhibitor syringe that became standard issue for all armed forces. He jabbed the syringe into the man's arm. Thus ending the man's feeble attempt of taking down the duo.

Meanwhile, the bullish man was back on his feet, but in severe pain. He charged forward with aggression seeking another chance to inflict pain on Shayne.

"Seriously?" Shayne said. He was a firm believer in not making the same mistake twice, a lesson the bullish man hadn't learned. Shayne dove to his left evading the attack. The man's momentum pushed him forward, right into the patch of ice Jackson used to get his opponent off his feet.

"Caution, wet floor!" Jackson repeated. The bullish man landed right next to his partner in crime. Jackson whistled as he jabbed the syringe into the man's arm.

Alicia Torres and the cameraman hurried forward towards the duo and praised them for their efforts. Jackson posed for the camera and made a statement while Shayne contacted the local G.U.A.R.D. unit to apprehend the intruders.

Alicia made her final statement and thanked the two men for their time. She couldn't stop singing their praises as she wrapped up her segment. "This is going to be our biggest episode yet!" Alicia said to her cameraman. "Thank you guys so much for doing this interview, even without the impromptu battle that took place, this was going to be our biggest issue."

Shayne and Jackson smiled at the pretty woman. "It was our pleasure," Shayne said respectfully. "You've got a lot of talent Ms. Torres. Pretty soon the whole world is going to know it!" Shayne extended his hand and Alicia accepted it.

"Dude, ask her out already!" Jackson whispered as the two men began walking away.

"It was an interview nothing more." Shayne replied.

"You know, for someone as smart as you are, you can be really dumb when it comes to women. She's obviously interested, ask her out!" Jackson insisted, but Shayne refused.

"You have to let me make it up to you!" Alicia blurted out. Her words caused the two young men to turn back around and face her.

"That isn't necessary," Shayne replied.

"Sure it is!" Jackson insisted. "What did you have in mind?"

"How about dinner later on tonight at my place?" Alicia asked. Her face indicated that she was extremely nervous to hear Shayne's reply.

Jackson's face turned into a grimace. "Sorry, I can't make it, I already have plans. But Shayne here doesn't. He'll see you there!"

Alicia's smile grew twice as wide, "Great, I'll text you the address!"

"Sounds good!" Jackson replied.

Shayne looked at his friend in disbelief, "You liar, you don't have any plans tonight."

The duo walked past the G.U.A.R.D. unit that had just arrived and made their way out of the building.

"Sure I do, I've got big plans," Jackson insisted.

Shayne knew Jackson was full of it, but he decided to humor his friend anyway. "What sort of plans?"

"Getting you ready for your date tonight!"

Jackson took a few steps in front of Shayne and whistled. He was proud of himself for fixing Shayne up with Alicia and taking down a few more criminals in the process.

Christian Green is the author of three other books; The League of Protectors: Dawn of a New Age, The League of Protectors: Fire and Ice, and The Blood in Their Veins. He is an avid reader of all things fantasy related. As a writer, Christian focuses on telling a compelling story that engages the audience and delivers captivating dialogue. He is known for adding small bits of information in each story that connects with characters from other stories. Christian currently lives in Illinois. He is working on the next part of his The Ascendants series and book two of The Blood in Their Veins series.

Communication

You can communicate with Christian at
http://www.christianragreen.com/

On Facebook at
https://www.facebook.com/pages/Christian-R-A-Green/1525407597741770

Or Twitter @cgreen2685